MARKED BY WEREWOLVES

PACKS OF THE PACIFIC NORTHWEST SERIES,
BOOKS 1-3

MEG RIPLEY

Disclaimer

This book is intended for readers age 18 and over. It contains mature situations and language that may be objectionable to some readers.

CONTENTS

MARKED BY WEREWOLVES

PART I
CLAIMED BY THE WOLF BROTHERHOOD

Chapter 1	5
Chapter 2	24
Chapter 3	48

PART II
WEREWOLF BABY DADDY

Chapter 1	59
Chapter 2	84
Chapter 3	92
Chapter 4	100
Chapter 5	112
Chapter 6	124
Chapter 7	134
Chapter 8	138
Chapter 9	149
Chapter 10	161

PART III
THE WOLF PACK'S REVENGE

Chapter 1	169
Chapter 2	179
Chapter 3	187
Chapter 4	204
Chapter 5	212
Chapter 6	218
Chapter 7	229

Chapter 8   233
Chapter 9   240
Chapter 10   251
Chapter 11   266
Chapter 12   271
Chapter 13   279
Chapter 14   293
Chapter 15   298
Chapter 16   303
Chapter 17   313
Chapter 18   317

MARKED BY WEREWOLVES

THE PACKS OF THE PACIFIC NORTHWEST SERIES

PART I

CLAIMED BY THE WOLF BROTHERHOOD

1

"Hey, Boss? There's some guy outside who wants to talk to you."

Aiza Simpson sighed and pulled her attention away from her spreadsheets. It was difficult to shift her attention from the maddening minutia of numbers and formulas, but this was the third interruption in thirty minutes, and it was probably time to accept she would not be balancing the bar's books that night.

"What guy? And what does he want to talk about?"

"A big guy." Cyn demonstrated by holding a hand far above her head and then her palms wide apart, miming a very big guy indeed. "Biker."

"What does he want?"

"He didn't say. He just told me he wanted to talk to you. I told him you were busy and that he could talk to Chad instead, but he said he had to talk to you."

She had no desire to speak to a big biker, but this was the third night a man matching that description showed up after closing time, demanding to see Aiza. Clearly, this asshole was not going to take a hint. Maybe if she got the meeting out of the way, the stranger would leave her alone and she would actually get some work done.

"Okay. Tell him I'll be right out."

"Actually, I think right here is just fine." A giant man clad in leather from head to toe pushed Cyn out of the way and filled the doorway. "Aiza Simpson, you're not an easy woman to find."

"I didn't know anyone was looking for me."

"Should I—" Cyn started.

Aiza waved her away. "Go finish up for the night and get home."

"Sure thing." She shot the stranger a suspicious look and then ducked past his shoulder and scurried from the office.

"So, Mr.—"

"Butch."

"Mr. Butch, what can I do for you? If you're

trying to book your band, you will need to speak with Chad. I don't handle any of that."

"It's just Butch, and no ma'am, I'm not trying to book a band."

"Well, have a seat." Aiza lowered herself to her chair, reminding herself that she owned the place and that this man could not intimidate her, even if he chose to remain standing, looming over her desk.

"I'm here to talk about your taxes." His voice was a low rumble that came from deep in his chest, and as he spoke, Aiza realized the left side of his mouth didn't move. Puckered flesh marked a scar that stretched from his nose to his chin.

"Taxes? You don't look like someone who works for the Internal Revenue Service."

"I work for the Brotherhood."

Aiza's mouth ran dry but she was careful to school her features, keeping her face completely calm. "Which brotherhood?"

"The Wolf Brotherhood."

"I've already told your associates that I will not be part of that racket."

"If you don't pay your taxes, how will we protect you and this lovely establishment?"

"I don't need protection. People come here

because they're looking for a good time. Your kind isn't welcome here."

Butch came around to her side of the desk, the heels of his boots thumping against the wood floor. He stood so close she had to tilt her head back to see his face, but she refused to lean back or move away from his great bulk. "This town belongs to the Brotherhood. And so does everything *in* this town."

"This bar belongs to *me*. If that's not clear to you, I'll be happy to call the cops and press charges for trespassing."

"Trespassing? Who's trespassing? I'm just here to have a little chat." He glanced down at her desk and his hand shot out without warning, knocking her computer to the ground. "But if you want to call the cops, you're welcome to."

"Nobody wants the cops involved. Just go tell your boss or your alpha or whatever that I'm not paying."

"Is that your final answer?"

"It's the only answer you're ever gonna get from me."

"That's a shame." He hooked his hand under her desk and flipped it like it was made of cardboard. The resulting crash was loud enough to make her jump, and all she could do was pray that the heavy wood hadn't landed directly on her laptop. Most of her information was backed up, but not the most recent updates to her spreadsheets.

He walked out of the room without another word and she followed quickly behind him, wincing as glasses, bottles, and plates fell to the ground in his wake. Two of her waitresses yelped and jumped at the unexpected crashes, and Chad watched the destruction with a gaping mouth, looking even more like an idiot than usual.

"Cyn, get this glass cleaned up. Chad, come back here and help me out."

He didn't need to be told twice, thankfully. He silently helped her right the desk and watched as she gingerly picked the laptop up from the ground. One of the hinges was broken, but the screen came to life and nothing else appeared to be damaged.

"How much did he want?" Chad asked.

"I don't know."

"What do you mean, you don't know? Didn't you ask?"

"Why would I ask?" Aiza said, gathering up the receipts and invoices that had gone flying. "I'm not paying any amount."

"What do you mean, *you're not paying any amount?*" Chad's voice had an undeniable tremor.

"Look, Aiza, I know you're new to all this, but he's going to come back. And when he does, he's going to want more. And they'll just keep coming back until they've taken everything."

"What are you saying? That I should just let them push me around and *extort* me? That I should write them a check? This isn't Chicago in the 1920s, Chad, this is 2016. I don't have to put up with that bullshit."

"It doesn't matter if it's 1916 or 2016. Men like that? They don't take no for an answer."

"Go see if Cyn needs any help. Then you can both go home for the night."

Chad opened his mouth like he had another argument, but Aiza was done with the conversation. She turned her back on him and pretended to be absorbed by her paperwork, but she couldn't see anything past the blurring of tears in her eyes. In the six months since she bought the controlling interest in Paul's Tavern, she'd been insulted, cheated, lied to, and harassed. She'd lost ten pounds and any memory she'd ever had of a good night's sleep. She no longer had personal days off, no longer had peaceful moments or pleasant dreams.

But all of it—the pain, inconvenience, sweat and tears—had been worth it. All she ever wanted was something she could call her own. Something she could build and nurture and hold up with pride. Every back-breaking minute of work proved her dreams were coming true—but now, every drop of blood and sacrifice she made could be wiped away by one piece of shit.

No, not just one. A whole pack of them. A whole *Brotherhood*.

"The shit Brotherhood," she muttered under her breath. Well, if the shit brotherhood thought they could take everything away from her without a fight, they had another thing coming. She'd go down swinging. She'd scrap and spar and scuffle until she had no strength left, and then she would fight a little harder.

First, she would need to prepare for their next meeting. She had no doubt Butch would return, as promised, and when he did, she would be ready for him. He might not take *no* for an answer, but a bullet would speak plenty loud, and it would get her message across, even to deaf ears.

When she emerged from the office, the bar was empty and the shards of broken glass had been cleared from the floor. She circled the small space, running her fingers over the smooth, well-worn tables and chairs, straightening the frames on the wall, dusting the tops of the light fixtures with the rags she always kept tucked in her belt.

"I'm not going to let anything happen to you," Aiza vowed. "I don't care what I have to do. Whatever it takes."

When she finalized the sale of the bar with Paul, he'd advised her to purchase a gun. Aiza had never been a fan of firearms, and she couldn't imagine herself killing another human being—well, at least until that night. Now she took great pleasure in picturing Butch's smirking face being torn apart by a well-timed bullet. She decided to look into getting a gun the next morning.

After another walk-through to make sure that everything that should be off was off, everything that should be on was on, and everything else was clean and secure, Aiza left through the service door, careful to pull it shut behind her. It wasn't raining, yet, but she could smell it in the air, and the sky was overcast, the heavy clouds colored orange by the city lights. Long after last call, the streets were deserted and the parking lot was empty—except for her little Honda.

She'd crossed that parking lot by herself a thousand times before in the ten years since she started there as a dishwasher. She'd moved from dishwasher to waitress to bartender to manager to owner in that time, and every day of that journey had been punctuated by that very walk, but now she couldn't quite bring herself to take the first step. She scanned to the left and then to the right, looking for any movement in the shadows, but she saw nothing. She heard nothing. Her senses told her the way was clear, but her instincts kept her by the door, screaming at her to go back inside, push the deadbolt, and call the cops.

Aiza was just about to silence those instincts when she heard it: nails scraping over concrete. A whisper of a sound that would have been lost during the day, drowned out by traffic and voices. But in the night, Aiza heard it as clear as a bell. She barely had time to register the sound before the shadows shifted and something lunged from the darkness. Her instincts kicked in before her training, and the world seemed to move around her as she shifted from two legs to four.

As a wolf, she was stronger, faster, and far more deadly, but the other wolf had a running start and hit her with enough force to drive her to the ground. She yelped and whipped her head around, her sharp teeth slashing through the air and finding just enough flesh to draw blood. It was the attacker's turn to yelp as she tightened her jaw, biting down with all her strength, tearing fur and flesh from the lean wolf's shoulder.

They broke apart, snarling. As a human, Aiza might have noticed that her opponent was far too big for her to take down. As a human, she might have noted the copious scars, the wounds he wore as marks of pride, signaling every fight he'd won. But as a wolf, all Aiza knew was that she had to protect her territory. The wolf lunged forward and Aiza leapt in the air to meet him, not willing to give Butch so much as an inch. She went low, aiming for his underbelly, but his long claws snagged her face, tearing a deep hole through her cheek. That didn't stop the trajectory of her attack, however, and her teeth sank into his stomach like hot knives through butter.

Aiza growled, whipping her head from side to side, using the full force of her weight to tear through his guts. Butch's howl was one of mingled pain and fury, but he somehow managed to wrap his jaws around her neck. At the first hint of pressure from those sharp points, Aiza released her hold and sprang back. Blood as black as oil poured from their open wounds, splattering across the parking lot like a gruesome Jackson Pollock painting.

Aiza felt herself growing weaker, but she didn't register any pain; didn't register the implications of her slower reflexes. All she knew was the taste of blood on her snout and the need to defend her territory at all costs. She might have paid the ultimate price, but the darkness around her shifted again as a gray wolf sprung through the air.

The newcomer landed on the back of Butch's neck, ripping him away from Aiza with a strong bite. The two wolves rolled across the ground, teeth flashing white, long legs flailing and tangling together. The newcomer found his feet first, and still unharmed, took advantage of Butch's weakening legs, burying his snout in Butch's throat and biting hard. The other wolf's howl was cut off, turning into a thick gurgling sound as blood poured from his throat and his mouth. The newcomer held him in place until he stopped twitching and his body went limp.

With the threat removed, Aiza shifted back to herself. She was exhausted, yet her nerves were screaming, sending her entire body on edge. She felt like she could run for miles; she wanted to scream and needed to work the excess energy out of her system. She stood on shaking legs, blood streaking down her naked skin. The gray wolf shifted as well, giving Aiza a perfect view of his finely muscled, familiar form.

He turned to her, shoulders rolling back, long hair blowing in the wind. Aiza's heart still raced, her chest rising and falling rapidly. He closed the length between them in two long strides, his strong fingers closing around her shoulders. His grip was tight enough to leave finger-shaped bruises as he lifted her feet off the ground, carrying her to the hood of her car.

Her legs wrapped around his hips automatically, pulling him against her welcoming body, and their mouths clashed. She tasted blood on his lips and tongue, and she knew he must have tasted the same coppery combination from her own mouth. His erection slid against her bare, soft thigh, and she felt the pulse of his heart pounding through his rigid flesh. He reached between them and guided his length to her opening.

He entered her in one long, hard stroke. They'd been silent except for their ragged breathing, but as soon as he filled her, they both cried out. She clenched around him, pulling him as close as possible, her head dropping back with pure relief. The entire car shook with the force of his thrusts, and her body absorbed the shock of his strength, sweat gathering on the back of her neck, rolling down her throat, smearing across his skin. A breeze picked up, rolling over her heated flesh, bringing her nipples into two tight peaks. His thumbs rolled over the nubs as he rocked into her, his mouth pulling into a smile as she moaned and bucked her hips.

Her fingernails raked over his shoulders and down his back as the flames of pleasure fanned through her. She gripped the back of his head and dragged his mouth back to hers, using the pressure of his lips to muffle her growing moans. His tongue moved against hers, and he snapped his hips in just the right tempo, pushing her closer and closer to the edge she was reaching for.

His mouth moved from her lips to the side of her neck, the tips of his sharp teeth playing over her slick skin; the pressure was enough to make her shudder. Once she started shaking, she couldn't stop, her body quaking with the power of her release. That was the moment his teeth sank down, and though the pressure was hard enough to leave a bruise, she didn't feel a second of pain; only pure sensation as the pleasure caught into an inferno, fueled by adrenaline from the fight and the endorphins always released when she shifted into a wild creature—a creature powerful enough to kill.

She howled as she soared over the edge, the sound carrying across the sleeping city.

"God, Dwight," she clutched his hair and pulled his head back, "why can't you ever be on time?"

"Get out of here before the cops come, Baby Doll."

"*You* get out of here. I'll talk to the cops," Aiza said, voice full of righteous fury. "That guy attacked me."

"No, Baby Doll, you're not talking to anybody." He released her and straightened. A moment later, he was moving to his motorcycle for his clothes. She shivered and looked around, but her clothes were not only out of reach, they'd been completely shredded by her sudden transformation.

"Bring me your jacket."

Dwight complied, fishing out a cigarette before handing it over.

Her face twisted with disgust as he lit it and took a long drag. "It's not your decision."

"It's my decision to keep my head attached to my shoulders," Dwight countered. "Butch was a pretty high-ranking member of the Wolf Brotherhood."

"All the more reason to talk to the cops," Aiza argued, shrugging the heavy leather jacket on. She'd never admit it, but she loved the way Dwight's jacket smelled—especially now that her senses were heightened by her lycanthropy. She could just imagine his smirk if he ever found out that piece of information.

"Either the cops give the Brotherhood a hard time and they retaliate by coming after you, or the cops tip off the Brotherhood that you're looking to give them a hard time and they come after you. They know he was here tonight."

Aiza's eyes narrowed. "And you knew he'd be here, too."

"Paul's Tavern is part of the regular route."

"Well it's not *Paul's* anymore—it's *my* goddamned tavern. That's it, first thing Monday morning, I'm changing the sign. After I buy a gun."

Dwight eyed the dead wolf. "You don't need a gun, Baby Doll."

"*You're* the one who killed him. You're just trying to save your own neck. You don't want the cops to tip off the Brotherhood to what really happened."

"And what really happened, Aiza?" He took her by the shoulder, his eyes boring into hers. "Is it that I saved your life?"

"Dwight—"

"There is a world of hurt waiting for you once they know about Butch. I'd just as soon avoid that, but hey," he raised his hands and smiled a smile that wasn't very warm, "it's up to you."

The thought of covering up a man's death—even if she didn't regret the death itself—made her sick to her stomach. She hadn't done anything but defend herself, but that defense was weakened considerably by an obstruction of justice charge. She'd lose everything if she went to jail. Her bar, her house, everything.

But none of that would count for much if she was dead.

"I'll go home."

"And you won't mention this to anyone."

Aiza shook her head, the sick feeling in her stomach growing worse by the second. "I won't mention this to anyone."

"Good girl." He hunted around the parking lot and found her purse. She accepted it with numb fingers and a nod of thanks.

"I'll be by later for my coat. Don't let anyone else in the house."

At that moment, she had no intention of letting *him* into her house. All she could think about was a stiff drink and a hot shower, but ultimately, neither quieted her nerves nor calmed her upset stomach.

Aiza's home was her sanctuary. The one place

the rest of the world couldn't touch her and wasn't welcome. She rarely invited friends, or boyfriends, to her home; her need for privacy was too great. Most of the time, her friends or boyfriends respected her boundaries and didn't press for more, but Dwight was neither a friend nor a boyfriend, and he had no reason to respect her boundaries.

She met Dwight at the bar while she was still waitressing. He was a regular and he tipped well, and though he wasn't her type at all, she still found herself responding to his flirtations and smiles. She never intended to sleep with him, and after she slept with him the first time, she didn't mean to sleep with him a second time—or a third time. It was a mistake. That's what she told him each time, and yet it appeared he was her favorite mistake to make because, like a moth to a flame, she just couldn't keep away from him.

Even after he turned her into a werewolf.

Especially after he turned her into a werewolf.

She inspected her home with the same care she used at the bar, checking the locks on her doors and windows and arming her security system. The security system was still new; she had it installed after her turning. Dwight had warned her that the Brotherhood forbade anyone in the pack from making new wolves, and though she didn't quite understand why that was *her* problem, she still took as many safety precautions as she could.

As soon as she secured the place, she stripped Dwight's jacket from her shoulders and climbed into a hot shower. The water turned pink as it ran down the curves of her body and pooled at her feet, but most of the blood had dried and needed to be scraped off with her loofah. Her injuries were minor and already beginning to heal, but they still stung under the hot water. Her eyes burned and tingled, but she blinked back the tears; there was no reason to cry. She was fine. She would continue to be fine.

Everything would be fine.

No matter how many times she repeated that to herself, she couldn't quite believe it.

Once she was out of the shower, she wrapped herself in her fluffy fleece robe and put the kettle on to boil water for tea. Her stomach growled with the same ferocity as a wolf and the accompanying pain drove her to the fridge. She was always horny and hungry after she shifted into her lupine form. Now that Dwight had satisfied one craving, she was left to prepare her own dinner. All she wanted was meat— lean, red, raw meat. She scanned the fridge and zeroed in on a pound of ground beef, deciding that a burger made very rare would fit the bill.

While her tea steeped and the burger cooked, she downed a double shot of good ol' Kentucky bourbon. It burned all the way down, but in a good way that left her skin flushed and tingling. Another double, and she started to feel somewhat normal. She fished her phone out of her purse to see if Dwight had called; he hadn't, but her sister, Sera, had.

She felt a familiar pang when she saw her sister's name. It had been years since they last spoke—not because Aiza didn't miss her or love her, but somehow, the longer she went without speaking to her family, the harder it was to call them.

So many things had changed, in both good and bad ways. What would she say? *I'm doing really well now. I have a house, a bar, and oh yeah, by the way, I'm a werewolf, and I just killed a man.*

"Tomorrow," she promised herself. "I'll give her a call tomorrow."

2

MOST NIGHTS, AIZA DREAMED ABOUT THE DAY SHE died.

She didn't remember being dead. She didn't remember the crash itself. Later, she was told they skidded to avoid an oncoming car, a drunk driver in the wrong lane. The blow she took to the head would have killed her instantly, if it wasn't for her helmet. It was still a big enough hit to knock her unconscious for three days and wipe several days from her memory.

For a full month, she had no ability to make new memories. She had to be reminded of her own name, her own life, every day. Even now, she had no recollection of those thirty days. She couldn't recall how frustrating and frightening it must have been.

Aiza tried to imagine the woman who had lived through that waking nightmare; tried to imagine what it must have felt like to be in a state of perpetual confusion.

She tried to imagine the woman who heard Dwight's offer and had no choice but to accept it.

She did remember the bite.

In the video Aiza made of herself, she explained that the bite would be serious enough to scar. He'd chosen the inside of her left thigh, and Aiza had spent a long time contemplating the placement of that bite. She hardly thought it would have been *her* first choice, so the placement must have been Dwight's decision.

She went on to explain that she would feel a strong connection to Dwight from then on, no matter what happened, no matter how much distance she tried to put between them.

Aiza had been perplexed by that statement— what *kind* of connection? Would she suddenly find herself in love with the man? Would she be enthralled by him?

The connection wasn't anything so awful or so simple.

"So, why am I doing this? Because it looks like it's my only chance. My only choice. The transformation from human to werewolf might repair the damage done to my brain. Dwight brought in a specialist who explained that werewolves have the ability to heal faster, and that ability is currently being studied all over the world. Doctors can't explain why, but there have been studies that demonstrate that humans who are infected with lycanthropy will show the alleviation and sometimes reversal of all kinds of things—including brain damage."

In fact, Dwight had been injured in the accident, too, but he had completely recovered in less than a week. He'd told her that he was walking again the day before she woke up.

The video also included footage of her discussion with the specialist, warning there were risks associated with the transformation, too. Aiza had studied the video countless times, watching the play of her face as the doctor explained the entire process, gave her the warnings, and told her how her life might change.

Dwight told her she'd watched the video every day for two weeks, and each day of those two weeks, she shook her head. Then, on the fifteenth day, she'd signed the paperwork to give Dwight legal permission to turn her into a werewolf. What had changed on that day? Aiza would never know. She'd also never truly know for sure that she had changed her mind. There was no independent verification of the moment she said *yes*—just Dwight's word.

But she didn't care too much, either. It had been the right thing to do, and her ability to make memories returned one week after the bite. Within a month of that, she was able to return to work at her newly-purchased bar. Fortunately, Paul had stayed on to run the place while she was recovering, and it was in perfect working order when she was ready to take the reins.

Unfortunately, stepping back into her life wasn't that easy, though. There were plenty of websites and even support groups to help her transition into her new life as a wolf, but many of the people in the support groups were literally victims, brutally attacked and changed against their will. She didn't feel comfortable revealing her own story and listening to everybody recounting how wolves ruined their lives frightened her. Would she always be able to control herself? Would she harm—even kill—someone someday?

Ultimately, Dwight was the only one she could speak to about her fears. A part of her almost expected him to shrug it off, but that was when she learned the meaning of the word *connection*.

Dwight had taken her concerns and fears seriously. He promised to teach how to change at will, how to control herself as a wolf, and how to handle her heightened senses. She didn't find herself falling in love with him, but she did enjoy the time she spent with him, even when they weren't having sex —and they had *a lot* of sex in between their lessons on meditation, concentration, and control.

Most mornings, when she woke up, the scar on her thigh throbbed and her head pulsed with the memory of that moment, when teeth sank into flesh and her blood mingled with his saliva, carrying the virus through her system.

Other than that, Aiza had reached the point where she rarely thought about being a werewolf. Her life was full, busy and healthy.

But now a threat hung over her life, and when she woke from the dream with a breathless gasp at half past three, she knew she wouldn't be getting back to sleep that night. Something had woken her. She strained her ears to listen for approaching footsteps.

"Dwight?" Her voice was barely above a whisper. "Is that you?"

"It's me, Baby Doll."

Light flooded the room and Aiza gasped as she saw that Dwight wasn't alone. The man pointing a gun at Dwight offered Aiza a cruel smile, "Hi, *Baby Doll*. It's a pleasure to finally meet you."

"Who...?" She couldn't take her eyes off the gun. "What's happening?"

"This is Franklin," Dwight said, his voice surprisingly even. "He's on the Brotherhood's counsel."

"What do you want?" Now that she was over her initial shock, anger flooded her system. Why couldn't these assholes leave her alone? She'd never done anything to them. Dwight had mentioned before that the Brotherhood strictly forbade creating new werewolves. She understood it was against their rules or whatever, but *she* was under no obligation to live under their rules.

"I just wanna chat. I have a few questions, that's all. And since Dwight refused to answer, I thought I'd get the news from the horse's mouth, so to speak."

"I have nothing to say to you," Aiza said as dismissively as she could.

"I thought you might say that. But I've had my eye on you for a while, Aiza Simpson, and I know something you don't know."

"Oh, really? What's that?"

"I know where your sister lives."

"So what?" Aiza asked, trying to keep her voice even, though he must have sensed the sudden increase in her heart rate.

"So maybe I'll make myself a mate like Dwight here did."

Aiza's mind flashed to the support group survivors, the ones who'd been held down and turned against their wills; the ones who were forced to feel an emotional and physical connection to the wolves who ruined their lives. She could not fathom Sera becoming one of them, and somehow, Franklin knew that Dwight had turned her, too, which meant that he was going to be in for a world of hurt once the rest of the Brotherhood found out.

"What do you want to know?"

"Where's Butch?"

"I don't know," Aiza answered. "I don't even know who Butch is."

"Don't lie to me, Aiza. It doesn't become you. Now I'm trying to have a decent conversation with you, but if you're not capable of that, I can find other ways to get the information I need."

"Why do you think I know anything about this Butch guy?"

"Because he had a meeting with you today," Franklin said.

"Oh, I see. You sent him to shake me down and when he didn't return, you assumed that I had something to do with that. Get out of my house, or I'm going to call the police."

The longer this ridiculous conversation went on, the more enraged she became. But her anger wasn't a raging inferno—it was a slow moving glacier, turning her blood to ice and freezing her nerves until her fear shriveled up on itself.

Franklin narrowed his eyes over the barrel of his gun. She could see another threat building behind his lips as his finger tightened on the trigger. Dwight chose that moment to strike, distracting Franklin with a blow to the back of the head. He swung around, prepared to shoot Dwight, but Aiza lost no time, transforming as she lunged from her bed to the interloper, hitting him with the full force of her weight.

By the time they reached the ground, her fangs were bared and her claws were extended. Her bottom jaw crushed the man's neck in such a way that his vertebrae shattered, sending razor-like splinters into his spinal cord, killing him instantly.

Dwight sighed. "Fuck, Aiza, what have you done now?"

Aiza released the man and licked her chops before shifting back to her human form. "What have I *done?* Why don't you go fuck yourself, Dwight! You brought this asshole to my *house.*"

"Well, what are we going to do with him?"

"Whatever you did with Butch, I guess."

"You have no idea what you've done," Dwight said.

Aiza was unperturbed. "I'd do it again."

"I don't doubt it. You need to get out of town."

"No." She folded her arms. "I'm not running."

"Do you think this is going to stop? Butch was just a foot soldier, but Franklin—"

"Was an asshole," Aiza supplied. "And I thought you said Butch was a high-ranking member?"

"They're both high-ranking enough to be missed."

"I'm not going anywhere until you tell me the truth. All of this bullshit today, it has nothing to do with me, does it?" Aiza asked.

"It's...complicated."

"Excuse me?" Aiza looked down at the growing blood stain on her carpet. It filled her senses, clogging her mouth and nose, painting her vision red. "What's so goddamned complicated?"

"Aiza, you're one of the Owned."

"The *Owned?*" The vein in her temple began to throb, sending a sharp pain through her skull to her eye. "What the fuck are you talking about?"

"I made you. The Brotherhood found out, but I was able to pull a few strings and smooth things over. Keep in mind, though, that everything I have belongs to the pack, and so—"

"And so *what?* I belong to the Brotherhood, too? Like a piece of property?"

"As far as they are concerned, yes."

She closed her eyes and took a deep breath, but only succeeded in filling her head with the smell of blood. "I'm going to kill you."

"Aiza, Baby Doll—"

"Don't. Don't call me that. Don't...just...just get out!"

"I can't. They're just going to keep coming. You are mine now, and they want what's theirs."

"This wasn't in the video. This wasn't in the paperwork. That...that isn't what I *agreed* to, Dwight. You fucking lied to me. What else did you lie to me about?"

She pushed herself to her feet and stumbled

backwards to the bed, trying to put as much distance between herself and Dwight as possible. Her stomach churned, generating bile that bubbled to the back of her throat. She tried to swallow it, but it lingered there, burning her esophagus.

"I didn't—"

"Don't talk. Don't tell me another lie." She shook her head. "You have to fix it."

"I don't—"

"Don't tell me you can't," she said sharply. "Don't tell me that I have to spend the rest of my life giving *them* everything. Being *Owned*. Is that—oh God, that's why he knows about my sister. They know everything about my family, don't they?"

Dwight only nodded.

"Get me out of this or I swear to God, I'll—"

"What?"

"I'll kill you," Aiza stated simply.

"You won't kill me."

She pulled herself to her full height and narrowed her eyes, summoning all of the wild courage of the wolf inside of her. Her lip curled and she felt the growl rumbling through her throat. "This is not an idle threat, Dwight. Those fuckers think my life belongs to them? Fine. But before they bring me down, I swear I will rip your throat out."

Dwight's attention shifted to the dead man at his feet and he didn't need to consider her words for long. "Aiza, you need to die."

"Is that a threat?"

Dwight shook his head. "It's a plan. We'll fake your death—"

"We'll what my *what?*"

"They can't come after you if they think you're dead."

Aiza blinked, unable to believe her own ears. "That solves nothing. If they think I'm dead, the whole world will think I'm dead. I'll lose my house, my bar. Goddamn you, Dwight, *goddamn you!*"

"We'll get your will in order and you won't lose anything. This is only going to be temporary."

"What are you talking about? Temporary? Do you think if I disappear for six months, they'll just forget about me? Who will run the bar?" Aiza looked down at the body. It was getting more and more difficult to concentrate with the scent of blood permeating everything. "Why did you do this to me? Why did you make me a wolf if you knew...if you knew this...how could..."

She couldn't finish her sentence. She couldn't even breathe. Her lungs were frozen; her throat clogged with ragged, sharp words.

Dwight crossed the room and took her by the shoulders. "You want to know how I could do this to you? Because I'm a selfish asshole. You surprised I'd admit it?"

"A little."

"Aiza, I visited you in the hospital every day. And every day, you looked at me with such...fear and confusion. You were afraid and you were hurting and there wasn't a damned thing I could do about it. Until the moment there was."

"But didn't you even think about the consequences? Didn't you even consider we could be here...like this...one day?"

"All I could think about was fixing you. Saving you. When I woke up in the hospital and I didn't know where you were, if you even made it, I never felt more sick in my life. I made the nurses take me to you and I stood there, watching you in that coma, and I knew if you pulled through, I would do anything for you."

Aiza took a deep breath, caught up in his dark eyes, looking for any hint of a lie. But he was telling her the truth. She could see it, and more importantly, she could feel it. The connection between them felt stronger than ever, and she unconsciously shifted towards him, seeking out the heat and strength of his body, her nostrils finally detecting his familiar scent through the ocean of blood.

"I know you think I fucked up," he continued, "but I wouldn't have done it any other way. I'd rather have you here yelling at me than not have you at all. Won't you forgive me?"

Aiza felt the sting of tears and tried to blink them away before they could fall. Her life was in shambles and she could trace all of it back to her decision to get involved with him—and yet she'd never felt closer to another human being. Worse still, she *wanted* to be close to him. She'd always wanted him. Now she had exactly what she wanted, she needed to handle the consequences.

"How...how are we going to do this? Stage my death?"

"We'll need a body and a story."

"A *body*?"

"Yeah, Baby Doll. You can't just disappear and expect that'll do the trick. The Brotherhood must believe you're dead and that your property reverted to me."

"Oh great. So they have to believe they won and I'll still lose everything."

"Just because they think it's mine doesn't mean it

will be mine," Dwight clarified. "I'll keep an eye on the bar and make sure you don't lose the house."

"Where will I be?" Aiza asked.

"Out of sight. I have friends in the county, they'll help me get everything pushed through and keep it quiet."

"What about the funeral? What about the burial? What about my family?"

Dwight's hand moved up her neck, his long fingers pushing the hair from her face. "Do you trust me, Baby Doll?"

That was a loaded question. Even before she became a wolf, she routinely put her life in his hands, especially when she climbed onto the back of his motorcycle. Now that she was a werewolf—*his* werewolf—trusting him felt like the only thing she could do. If she didn't have her maker, who did she have? None of her friends even knew she was a wolf and her family would only take the news as yet another sign that she was a fuck-up.

She didn't know how to answer with words, so she closed her eyes and nuzzled into his touch. His fingers widened, spreading across her scalp, and he cradled her head gently. His warmth seeped into her skin, and so did the undeniable sense that every-thing was going to be alright. She didn't know where that feeling was coming from—if she truly felt it or if he was sending her that soothing sensation—but she didn't care.

When he tilted head to claim her mouth with a gentle kiss, she didn't resist. They rarely kissed, and when they did, it was usually a hungry, desperate caress, as though they were trying to devour each other. There was hunger in this kiss, too, but it was tempered, as though he was waiting for a sign from here. With all the death and chaos, madness and confusion, kissing him—and inviting him to do more—seemed like it could wait.

And yet, it couldn't.

She parted her lips, inviting him to deepen the kiss, pulling his tongue in her mouth as she buried her fingers in his long hair. He hesitated for a moment—just long enough to make her worry that he might release her completely—and then she felt the full force of his passion and desire ricochet through her.

He lowered her to the bed, his hands working over her body, removing her stained clothes. Everywhere he touched her lit up, and goosebumps covered her from head to toe. She shivered again and again, not with the chill of the night air, but with the anticipation of more. More than just the sensation of his fingers flowing over her skin. She wanted him to grab her, to hold her; she wanted to feel him claim her again.

Her hands were busy, too, moving to his fly and trying to pull the zipper free. Her fingers felt cold and clumsy, and his dick bulged against the tight denim, making it even more difficult to work the zipper down. Finally, his larger hand closed over hers, fingers grabbing the tab and guiding it, freeing his engorged flesh. She wrapped her hand around his length, fresh excitement pulsing through her veins as she stroked him.

"God, look what you do to me," Dwight moaned, his mouth near her ear, his voice as hot and exciting as his touch. She squirmed beneath him, arousal flooding her system, making her wet; making her ache. She guided him to the juncture of her thighs, letting his swollen head slide between her lips, wetting his skin. The tip brushed against her clit, sending a shockwave up her spine. "I need to feel you."

He wasn't just saying that, either. She *felt* it; felt his desire flowing through him, fanning the sparks into flames—the flames that always threatened to consume her. Somehow, knowing it would consume him, too, made it all the better; made it easier for her to surrender to that passion. She guided his dick to her entrance, shifting her hips to take him inside of her. It was like touching a live wire to a dry pile of tinder—the sparks immediately caught and his name tore from her throat like a howl.

"Fuck me," she bit out. "Fuck me hard. God...hard...harder...."

He did as she asked, slamming his hips into her, his face set in lines of brutal concentration. She grasped at his arms, fingers digging deep into his flesh, silently begging him for more and more. She wanted to be free from her thoughts, free from the decisions and fears and from every conscious and self-conscious reaction. She didn't want to think about the past or the future, didn't want to consider what could happen—*didn't want to remember what she'd done.* When she turned herself over to him, to the pleasure their bodies could generate when they came together, she felt free.

But she wasn't quite there. Not yet.

Wrapping herself around him, holding him deep in her body, she gasped out, "Flip over."

He rolled onto his back, pulling her with him, and she rose above him, her hands flat on his chest for balance. His t-shirt irritated her fingers and she clawed at the material until it was gone, allowing her to feel the smooth expanse of his skin; the power of his muscles straining beneath her. His hands went to her full hips, pulling her down to meet every upward thrust. She rocked against him, grinding her clit into his pelvis, building on each aching second.

Through it all, she still could smell and taste blood. Her mind was clouded, so whose blood it was and why she could sense it didn't truly distract her from her goal. In fact, it only augmented her hunger, adding a sharp edge to every sensation until it sliced through her body. Each rock of her hips, each deep breath, every inch where skin moved against skin, where muscles flexed against muscles, each pull of her breath all coalesced into a sharp point of pleasure deep inside of her. That point pulsed brighter, hotter, and longer until it could no longer be contained.

The explosion it ignited rocked through her body, shaking her from her head to her toes. She screamed Dwight's name, grasping him tightly as she rode out each relentless crest of pleasure. Distantly, she heard his own ragged gasp, felt his dick jerk and twitch inside of her as he followed her over the edge and past the point of no return.

The high she got from him was always so intense, but short-lived. Caught up in that wonderful twilight between pleasure and the real world, she collapsed on top of him and tried to hold on for as long as she could, but gradually her breathing and heart rate returned to normal, and the world she wanted to ignore pushed down on her mind and her shoulders. Reality was an unwelcome visitor, intruding on her before she was ready to accept any guests.

"Pack only what you need," Dwight said, as though she needed his help to be pulled back to Earth. "We're getting out of here now."

Aiza nodded. What else was there to say?

But I'm not ready to go, her inner voice protested. *I'm not ready to let everything go. I'm not ready to walk away from my life. Don't do this.*

But what choice did she have? She inhabited a new world where she didn't know any of the rules and she had only one friend. If she wanted to stay alive in that world, adjustments had to be made. Sacrifices had to be made. If she wanted to stay alive at all, she would have to sacrifice everything she worked for.

As long as there's life, there's still hope, she promised herself. The world beat her down once before, but it couldn't keep her down. She'd fought her way to the top of every mountain she met, and if she had to do it again, she would. She would always keep fighting, but from now on, she would use greater care in picking her battles.

And her allies.

For the second time in a single night, Aiza fled the scene of a crime and left Dwight to handle the gristly details. She'd never been to his cabin, but he gave her directions and an explicit warning to go directly there, to speak to nobody else, and to keep her head down. She'd nodded, agreeing to follow his orders, quietly packing a small bag and resisting the urge to call Cyn. She couldn't tell her head waitress why she was disappearing or where she was going, but she desperately wanted to leave her a brief message. *Don't worry. Everything will be okay. Just keep the bar running and I'll be back soon.*

But even a message as simple as that could blow their entire story and ruin the plan they carefully worked out, once her head was clear again. It wasn't an easy plan, but it was simple. Straight-forward. All it required from her was her silent cooperation. All she had to do was drive away.

Now that the fever in her blood had cooled and the wave of emotions coming from Dwight had dulled, many of her previous trepidations returned. She couldn't shake the thought that she was handing it all over to Dwight; handing it all over to the Brotherhood. He swore he would keep it safe-guarded and wouldn't allow anyone else in the Brotherhood to come sniffing around, but she simply did not know if she could trust that—if she could believe him—if she *should* believe him.

She didn't reach the cabin until dawn. By then, her eyes were sore and gritty, her mouth was dry, and her bladder was uncomfortably full. She wanted nothing more than a hot shower and a soft bed.

The shower was exactly as she imagined it would be—better, even. She stood under the delicious spray for at least an hour, letting the water cleanse her of the blood and her exhaustion. She fell into the bed still wrapped in the towel, her heavy eyes falling the moment her head hit the pillow.

When Aiza woke up, she was dead again.

The car skidded out of control, according to the brief report on the local nightly news. Unable to correct the skid on the wet, rural road, the driver slammed into a utility pole and died instantly. They briefly flashed a picture of Aiza and then continued on to report that the number of traffic incidents on that particular stretch of highway was climbing steadily, and the local community was demanding for something to be done.

Although the story was exactly as she and Dwight had worked out, the shock of *seeing* it made her hands go numb and her breath hitch in her throat. The echoes of her actual accident made the scar on the back of her head throb, and she tried to ignore the tremor in her fingers, but it traveled up her arm and down to her legs.

The only thing Aiza didn't know—and didn't *want* to know—was who was actually in the car when it crashed. Dwight had brushed off her questions during the planning stage, and she had allowed him to do that, with the feeling that the less she knew, the better. That way, she could tell herself that "the body" he needed to locate was truly just a body and not, as she feared, a woman who looked like her, talked like her, and had been alive, just like her, only the morning before.

With the wheels of the plan set in motion, there was nothing for her to do but wait.

Dwight attended her small funeral—only her closest family was in attendance. There was another memorial for her, though, at the bar, and Dwight attended that, too. Aiza hadn't asked for any of the details. She felt too guilty, the weight of the lie only compounded by every friend, every family member, every associate and customer, and every stranger who heard of her accident and felt any sense of grief over her loss.

What she did not count on during all their quick planning was the tenacity and loyalty of her sister, Sera, who insisted on staying after the funeral to see to the house and Aiza's belongings; who went from bar to bar, apparently searching for Dwight or any possible lead or clue that would explain Aiza's untimely death.

3

"If your sister doesn't leave soon, we're going to have problems," Dwight warned, keeping his voice even.

He was doing his best not to demonstrate his extreme irritation at this unexpected development. Aiza never talked about her family. She was like Dwight—alone, without a pack, without burden. That had made her ideal for his purposes. And now some stranger was mucking up all his plans, causing ripples and pissing people off.

Even worse, she couldn't take a hint. He'd tried twice to scare her out of town, and it seemed to have the opposite effect. She finally fled Portland, but Dwight had the feeling that the bitch wasn't done sticking her nose where it didn't belong.

"Why? You made it look enough like an accident, and you said you had friends in the sheriff's department and the coroner's office," Aiza pointed out.

"I don't think she's going to uncover the plan or expose you. But..."

"But what? What are you worried about?"

"I want all of this to die down," Dwight said reasonably. "We need the Brotherhood to forget about you, forget about Paul's Tavern, and forget about the whole situation. They can't forget about it if she keeps telling people all over town that she thinks they murdered you."

Or, as it happened, if she continued to tell everybody around town that *he* was involved in her untimely death. He liked to keep a low profile anyway, but in this delicate situation, a low profile was absolutely paramount.

"I don't know what I'm supposed to do about it," Aiza said with a sigh. "I just want her to go home. I just want her to be safe."

"I'll take care of it," Dwight promised, with the same tone of reassurance and confidence he used since the whole nightmare started.

Ultimately, he intended for Aiza to accept him completely and without reservations as her Alpha. When she did, her regular note of contrariness would dissipate and he'd be able to guide her without resorting to planting a suggestion. But she hadn't accepted him yet, and so sometimes he had to take extra steps.

"C'mere, Baby Doll."

Dwight loved the way Aiza felt when he held her in his arms. He loved the way her curvy body fit against his. He loved the shape of her mouth and her eyes and her unbelievable spirit. He loved her body, loved fucking her; loved having her to himself. And he loved the way she gave everything over. *All he had to do was look her in the eyes.*

In fact, when he looked her in the eyes, he could make her do or say or think nearly anything he wanted. There were many things she didn't know about being a made wolf, though she thought she had an understanding of their new dynamics. He answered her questions and told her mostly the truth, but it was best if she didn't know it all. Best for him, at any rate.

With her gaze locked on his and his arms wrapped around her in a tight cage, he said, "Your sister is in the way."

She raised an eyebrow but then a blank look suddenly filled her eyes. "My... my sister is in the way," she repeated in a monotone voice.

"She needs to be removed."

"I don't want her to be *removed*," Aiza protested, her voice gaining strength. Despite himself, he felt a twinge in his chest. She had such a strong, beautiful will. She was one of the few people who challenged him and had no fear. Subduing her spirit and making her into his wolf had been all the sweeter for that. "I want to see her. I want to tell her the truth."

"You can't see her," Dwight said softly but firmly. "If you see her, you'll know she needs to die. You'll want to kill her."

He didn't feel a twinge of guilt at planting the suggestion in Aiza's mind. Sera Simpson was a complication Dwight hadn't counted on when he cooked up his plan to have both Aiza and Paul's Tavern completely under his thumb.

And now Sera had an unlikely ally in Seth Longtail, a tenacious Alpha from a rival pack. In his gut, Dwight knew that bringing Seth into the situation was a critical flaw in his master plan. The rival wolf Dwight chose to sacrifice to the Brotherhood—in exchange for his own punishment by death for turning Aiza—belonged to Longtail's pack, which meant that Seth wasn't going to stop sniffing around until he found the body or until Dwight took his life. One more death on his conscious would make no difference to him at this point, but as a matter of pure practicality, he didn't want to add the death of a powerful Alpha to his plate.

"I...I don't..."

"You want to kill her," Dwight repeated firmly, looking deeply into Aiza's eyes. "When you see her, you'll know she is trying to take it all from you. When you see her, you will remove her."

"But she's my sister."

"She wants to hurt you. She wants to hurt me. She wants to take me away from you. She doesn't want you to be happy and so you will remove her."

"I—I will remove her," Aiza repeated slowly.

"And when she's gone, we can be happy together," Dwight added. "When she's gone, you can go home again."

"I can go home again," she said faintly.

"Now, Baby Doll, do you want to please me? Do you want to make me happy?"

Aiza nodded, eyes blank, face open, her mind ready for more suggestions. Dwight hesitated, feeling a little overwhelmed by all the options. He made a wolf once before, and he used her until he literally broke her. He wanted things to be different with Aiza. He wanted to groom her and mold her into the perfect mate for him. He wanted to have her at his side, tucked away in his secret haven, for years to come.

He hadn't anticipated things turning into such a shit-show. He had no idea Franklin had his own designs on the goldmine that was Paul's Tavern and never expected him to send his henchman, Butch, to muscle in on Dwight's territory. His plan for Aiza was slow, designed for the long-game, meant to work past all of her defenses and shields until he was completely inside of her life, her head, and her heart.

After that point, she would be easy to control. Easy to exploit. But of course, an idiot like Franklin wouldn't appreciate a plan as subtle as Dwight's; he wouldn't be able to understand that it was better to have constant and open access rather than a tiny portion of the bar's income.

"She's going to come here, Aiza. She's going to try to take you away from me." He touched the side of her face. "Do you want to leave me, Baby Doll?"

"I don't want to leave."

"Good."

He kissed her, breaking eye contact. He couldn't keep her under suggestion at all times—not yet, anyway. The more he reinforced the bond between them, the easier it would be to keep her enthralled, but if he pushed for too much, too fast, he might cause damage. And he had absolutely no intention of harming his beautiful Aiza. Not when she was worth so much to him intact.

"Okay, Baby Doll, I've got to go. I have some business to take care of tonight. You stay here, and remember what I said."

She blinked at him with confusion and then nodded slowly. "I'll remember."

"What will you do if you see your sister?"

"I'll kill her," Aiza stated.

Dwight gave her a brief hug and another kiss on the top of the head before leaving. Once she killed her sister, she would have no strong ties to anyone except him. He had to admit, that was quite the unexpected boon. He'd been irritated ever since Sera arrived in town, but he couldn't complain about his opportunity to fully secure Aiza in his grasp— and due to Sera's unexpected involvement, he'd be able to complete his plan far sooner than he ever expected.

Dwight stepped outside of his cabin and inhaled deeply, catching the scent of an unfamiliar wolf floating in the wind. The hair on the back of his neck rose and his fangs emerged. Longtail had been there, and was most certainly still in the area.

Whistling to himself, he crossed the yard to the two-ton pickup truck he rarely drove. He preferred his bike to any other mode of transportation, or barring that, running freely as a wolf. But he needed something a little bit bigger than a motorcycle to get this job done.

With a cigarette clamped between his teeth and music blasting from his speakers, he put the truck into gear and roared into the night. With the window down, his sensitive nose guided him through the forest. Even with the stench of the cigarette, he wouldn't miss the smell of two wolves and one delicious human. He would know Sera was Aiza's kin by her scent alone.

He wondered if Sera would taste like her sister, too.

If he played his cards right, he'd have the chance to find out. Maybe he'd even have the chance to make Sera and keep her as well. Two sisters to do his bidding and serve his every need? Dwight's grin turned wicked, his thoughts turning feral as he descended upon his prey.

PART II

WEREWOLF BABY DADDY

1
_____

WALKING THROUGH AIZA'S HOME WAS LIKE PASSING
through a stranger's house. Sera recognized nothing
of her sister in the decor, the personal items, or even
the photographs. Aiza had been a dark-haired child
of just eighteen when she left their parents' home,
and the woman in the photographs was blonde,
fifteen years older, and hiding a lifetime of pain in
her eyes. Sera had come to Aiza's little bungalow in
Portland to find something, anything, that might
shed some light on her sister's life—and death—but
so far, the only thing she'd learned was that she truly
knew nothing about her eldest sibling.

Sera composed the obituary on the plane. She
emailed it to the *Portland Press Herald* and posted it
on her sister's social media accounts, but only her

closest family attended the funeral: their parents, Sigfreid and Judy, and their younger brother, Steven. There might have been another among the bereaved: a stranger who stood at a distance in the cemetery. Nobody else noticed him, but Sera had caught him out of the corner of her eye. In the fading light, she saw a ragged scar carving his face into uneven halves. Thick, bushy eyebrows shaded his eyes and a long, silky mustache flowed past his chin, almost to his neck. He'd been in full leather gear, and as he turned away, she caught a flash of a badge stitched onto his left sleeve: the profile of a wolf's body against a full yellow moon.

The sign of the Wolf Brotherhood, Sera came to learn. Most wolf packs were complex families with complicated lines linking them to their allied packs, but not the Wolf Brotherhood. They rode without allies, and any wolf banished from their own pack found a home among the Brotherhood. No crime barred them from membership; no wolf was too wild or too dangerous. As long as they swore their oath to the Alpha, they were welcome to ride with them.

Sera had found a badge just like the stranger wore in Aiza's belongings. To her, that pointed to a connection clearly worth pursuing, but the local sheriff's department disagreed with her on that.

"They were associates. That's not evidence. Besides, there were no signs of foul play. There wasn't even anything suspicious in the coroner's report." Sheriff Daniels offered a small, placating smile. "I know how upset you are. I know this is very painful and difficult to process, but it was an accident. Sometimes accidents happen when it's wet and dark."

Accidents did happen. Bad things happened to good people all the time. Lives were cut short without warning for the stupidest reasons and there wasn't a damned thing anybody could do about it. Sera couldn't deny any of that.

But in her heart, she couldn't accept it. Aiza deserved better.

Sera parted ways with her family in the cemetery. Siggy and Judy had cut short a cross-country trip, parking their RV in Chicago and flying back to Portland. They had a plane to catch and Steven's wife was just about to have a baby.

"I'm sorry. I'd stay and help you out with everything, but she's going to pop at any moment," Steven said.

Sera gave her little brother a long, long hug. She hadn't seen him in years—not since she left for college—and he was already grown up, with a job, and a wife, and a *baby*. She felt a familiar twinge in her heart at the mention of a baby, but it was flooded under the sadness and confusion she felt for her sister.

"Go to your wife." She squeezed him and stepped back, "I took the week off so I could take care of everything."

"I can come back. I'm only an hour away."

"I'll call you if I need you," Sera promised, knowing she wouldn't end up making that call.

Aiza had never been the easiest person to get along with, but Sera always had a special relationship with her sister. Even after she left home, the two had stayed in touch for years until one day, Aiza simply stopped answering her phone. She didn't return letters, didn't respond to emails, or even send out a Christmas card. Sera had feared the worst long before the phone call actually came and confirmed it. Now all she could do was try to find some sort of closure.

But as she picked her way through Aiza's home and her closest belongings, she began to realize that there would be no closure. Not until she satisfied her curiosity once and for all.

Her first step was to track down the scarred man.

There'd been no time to snap his picture, but

Sera found two photographs of him in Aiza's night-stand, tucked away under her a stack of bills and old magazines. One picture was of the two of them with wide smiles, taken a few months before. Sera stared at that picture for a long, long time, trying to find a hint of the girl she used to know.

The other picture was of the man by himself, sitting on a brand new motorcycle. He wasn't smiling at the camera, but the light in his eyes couldn't be missed. Neither picture had a name or any other identifying information, but it was a start.

With nothing but the pictures in hand, Sera set out to scour Portland for a clue—*any* clue. Aiza had kept several social media accounts, but none of them offered any clues about the scarred stranger. The bars were probably her best bet. Sera learned quickly that ordering a drink and greasing the bartender's palm helped make the experience more pleasant, though the first two nights were entirely unsuccessful. The bartenders, waitresses and bouncers would talk to her, but they wouldn't give her any helpful information.

Sorry, honey, never saw him.

Nope, don't know him.

He hasn't been around here.

By the third night, Sera's optimism was fading,

and so was her patience. She had the same feeling in her gut she had when she talked to the sheriff—the same feeling she always got when somebody looked her in the eye, smiled, and lied right to her face. It almost didn't seem worth it to go out and try again, but when she glanced at the photo and saw her sister's smiling face, Sera knew she didn't have a choice. Somebody had to be Aiza's champion. Somebody had to fight for justice.

The day was sunny, but clouds started to gather by twilight. A full moon loomed that night, but there were too many clouds to see the silver disc. When Sera hit the first bar, it was raining, and by the time she stepped out of the fifth bar, her coat was soaked through, her hair was a mess, and she was buzzed.

"No more beers," she muttered to herself as she jammed the key into the ignition. "Stupid rain," she added as she pulled out of the parking lot. Her fingers felt like ice, and even with the heater on full blast, she couldn't get warm. Rain splattered against the windshield, hitting it faster than the wipers could push it away, and the heat of her breath slowly fogged the glass, further obscuring her vision.

She slowed to a crawl, leaning forward and squinting through the fat raindrops slamming against her windshield. The headlights did little to slice through the darkness, and as much as she didn't want to give up for the night, she knew it would be best to find a safe place to park and sit this one out.

With that decision made, she signaled and looked for any parking lot or turn off to get her off the road. Staring intently to her right, she didn't notice the creature darting across the road from the left until it was too late to swerve out of the way. Her foot went to the brake, but the pedal barely depressed before she felt—and heard—her car collide with a body.

Sera jammed the car into park and paused, trying to catch her breath, her heart beating so hard she thought it might burst up through her throat. "Please don't be a dog. Or a deer. Please, please, please..."

She threw open the door and ducked her head against the rain, hurrying to the body lying under her bumper. Not a deer. Definitely not a dog. The prone body under her car was a man. A very tall— very naked—very gorgeous man. She couldn't see much in the furious storm, but she could see that much just fine.

"Mister? Hey sir? Sir? Hello? Hello! Mister! Wake up! Come on, oh, please wake up!" She gently slapped his face, but he didn't respond. "Oh God, please don't be dead. Please don't be dead."

She pressed her fingers to his neck, searching for a pulse and sobbed with relief when she felt it, strong and solid against her fingertips. His pulse was regular, as was his breathing, and she didn't see any signs of blood in the flickering light. That didn't rule out a serious head injury, but at least he was unlikely to die from the impact.

Sera straightened and took stock of the situation. The storm gave no sign of fading. She definitely couldn't leave the poor man on the side of the road and she had no idea where the nearest hospital was. She should call 911, but the police would certainly be dispatched, and Sera didn't want to talk to them.

She didn't see the streak of lightning, but the thunder was so loud it made her teeth vibrate. *Good God, girl, don't you know enough to get out of the rain?*

She bent her knees, squatting beside her unfortunate victim and hooked her hands under his arms. Sera's frame was short but powerful. She visited the gym daily, a habit she began five years earlier as a freshman in college. She could deadlift her own body weight—two-hundred and eighty pounds— and she was able to half-lift, half-drag the stranger from beneath the car and to door. From there, she hefted him into the back seat, tucking and folding his long limbs under the spare blanket she kept in the backseat.

Sera had no idea where she was, especially in relation to Aiza's house. Taking a naked stranger back there seemed out of the question anyway. Her phone told her there was a motel only a mile further down the road; all she had to do was drive in a slow, straight line and not hit any more men, and she would be fine.

Under normal circumstances, she would have been no more than five minutes away from her destination, but nearly thirty excruciating minutes passed before she saw the pink neon light through the rain. The *vacancy* sign flashed like a beacon, drawing her right up to the front door.

She worried the man behind the front counter would try to speak with her, but the exchange was mostly silent as he swiped her credit card, produced her room key, and explained she would need to drive around the corner of the building and park in the back.

Sera found a parking spot right next to her room door and sent a quick prayer of thanks to whichever deity or saint was in charge of such things. She propped the room's door open, turned the heater on full blast, and grabbed all the threadbare towels in the room before considering how to move him.

She couldn't drag his naked ass across the payment, so she pulled him into a seated position and then braced herself and lifted him into a fireman's carry. She kept her footing and her balance under his extra weight, making it all the way to the bed, and managed to lower him to the mattress before collapsing in exhaustion.

"Good job. Now what's the plan?" Sera muttered.

Getting dry. Getting warm. And getting this man to wake up. She promised herself if she couldn't rouse him to consciousness by morning, she would call the paramedics. His pulse was still strong, his breathing steady, and under the bright, even light she didn't even see a mark on him. She let her eyes linger over his body perhaps a fraction longer than necessary before covering him with a blanket, but even after he was covered, she couldn't stop looking at his perfectly proportioned, flawless body.

A small coffee maker sat by the sink and Sera brewed herself a pot, feeling a hundred times better once she downed a cup of the hot liquid. Suddenly, the man moved as if roused by the smell, and she gently slapped first one cheek then the other, trying to pull him back into the waking world.

"Mister? Mister, can you hear me? Hey, come on guy, wake up. Wake up!"

His eyes flew open and his arm swung wide. She barely had enough time to duck the blow, scurrying to get out of his reach. His gaze darted around the room as he took in his surroundings and finally settled on her.

"Who the hell are you?"

She licked her lips. "My name is Sera."

"Where the hell am I?"

"The Shangri La Motel."

He held the back of his head and squinted at her. *"Shangri La?"*

"Yeah, pretty cheesy, but it was the closest motel."

"The closest motel to what?"

"Um, well... How are you feeling?"

"My head hurts, but I'm alright." He explored the back of his head with his fingertips. "I've got a pretty nasty bump."

"I'm sorry about that. You ran in front of my car and I didn't see you until it was too late. You might have hit your head on the road."

"You hit me with your car and brought me to a friggin *motel*? Why not the hospital?"

"I—I don't know where it is, and it's raining

pretty bad. Plus, I wasn't sure if a man in your...*condition* wanted the authorities to get involved. But we can call the paramedics now if you want; I was going to call them in the morning if you didn't wake up."

The man started to shake his head and grimaced with pain. "No, it's fine. Were there any other damages? You weren't hurt, were you?"

"No, no, I'm fine. The car is fine. I was going pretty slowly. I don't even think I hit you that hard. Do you want some water?"

"That coffee smells great."

Sera nodded and poured the remaining coffee in the second Styrofoam cup and started brewing another pot.

"Thanks," he said as she passed over the cup. "You wouldn't happen to have any food, would you?"

"No, but we could order a pizza."

He nodded. "I like the way you think. I'm Seth, by the way."

"Nice to meet you, Seth. What do you like on your pizza?"

"Pepperoni."

"Pepperoni? Is that all?"

"I'm a man of simple taste."

Sera shrugged. "Fine with me."

She was happy to order the pizza, as it gave her

an opportunity to concentrate on something besides Seth. He seemed unconcerned by his naked state—he didn't even fix the blanket, and she could see every line of his chiseled stomach and hips.

Looking away from the lower half of his body only brought her attention to his face. His eyes were a warm shade of gray, his lips were full and the most alluring pink, and his strong jaw was covered with black stubble. Long black curls framed his face, softening the edge of his jaw and aquiline nose, and she wanted to comb her fingers through each one.

"Sera, how did you get me in here?"

"I carried you."

"You carried me? All by yourself?"

"Yeah. Does it surprise you that a girl can be strong?"

"No," he answered quickly. "No, not at all. It's just, you're so...short."

"I am short," she agreed amicably, "but I can bench press two hundred pounds."

Seth whistled between his teeth. "Remind me not to piss *you* off."

"This is your reminder." They exchanged a grin and Sera added, "Seriously, though, are you okay? Do you need a doctor? Would you like some ice for your head?"

"I'm fine. I'm mostly just hungry. Starving, actually."

"Can I ask, what were you doing running around in a rainstorm naked? Is that how you get your rocks off or something?"

"Well, I wasn't exactly running around naked; I do have a bit more sense than *that*. And I wasn't just out there for the fun of it. When you hit me, did you happen to see if anyone was following me?"

Sera shook her head. "I didn't see anyone else, but the rain was coming down pretty hard."

"Hopefully I lost them and they didn't follow me here."

"Lost *who*?"

"No one."

"You just said they could have followed you here. If that's the case, I think I have the right to know who might come knocking on my door."

Seth inclined his head. "Fair enough. The Wolf Brotherhood." He smiled wryly at Sera's sharp intake of breath. "I take it you've heard of them?"

"Yeah. You could say that. I'm looking for one of the wolves, actually."

"Well, you should stop looking for him."

"I can't do that."

"Trust me. A nice girl like you has no business tangling with people like that."

Sera shook her head. "I'm not tangling with anybody, I just need some information about my sister. Here, wait a second." She dug through her purse, producing the photos. "This is who I'm looking for. Do you know him?"

Seth didn't answer right away but she saw the flicker of recognition in his eyes as he studied the picture. "Never seen him."

"Really?"

He passed the photo over to her. "Really."

"Seth, I know we just met and we don't really know each other, so I hope you don't think I'm terribly rude when I call you a liar." She sighed. "Let me level with you. I don't know how, but I know this man was involved in my sister's death. I just need to ask him some questions about the night she died."

"I'm sorry for your loss," Seth said softly. "And I don't think you're terribly rude, though I'm not lying. I've never met the man, but I think I know his name: Dwight Lance."

"Thank you." Sera placed the photo back into her purse. "And thanks for the name. That's the most I've got in three days of looking."

"Looking? Are you showing that picture around town?"

"Do you know a better way to find a man?"

"I know that you don't want the whole world knowing you're looking for *that* particular man."

Sera frowned. "Why? Do you think he's dangerous?"

"I think Mr. Dwight Lance might come looking for you once he hears you're beating the bushes for him."

"Good. It'll save me a trip."

"You want the werewolf who may have been involved in your sister's death to hunt you down?"

Sera lifted her chin. "I'm not afraid of that bastard."

"I can see that. I'm just advising you to be careful."

"Sounds like you should have taken your own advice. What did you do to get the gang on your tail?" At his hesitation, Sera added, "Maybe if you talk about it, I can help."

"Two of my pack mates went missing. The last anybody heard from them, they were here in Portland. Their trail led me right to the Brotherhood's front door, but the Brotherhood doesn't take kindly to questions from strangers; that's why I think you ought to tread carefully."

"Pack mates? You're a *wolf*?"

"Yes. And I'm not leaving Portland until I get to the bottom of what's happened to them."

"Sounds like we're chasing the same trail. Maybe we should team up."

Seth arched his eyebrow. "You're pretty trusting."

"More like the enemy of my enemy is my friend. Besides, you haven't given me a reason not to trust you."

A sharp knock on the door made them both jump.

"It's just the pizza," Sera said, grabbing her wallet. She didn't look through the peephole, and Seth's shouted warning came a second too late as she twisted the lock. Thee knob turned violently in her hand the door slammed open, knocking her back several feet. In the blink of an eye, the man on the other side shifted into a wolf and lunged for her throat.

Sera automatically put her arms up to defend herself, but it was too little, too late. The wolf's weight and momentum knocked her to the ground and the beast snapped furiously at her face, the long muzzle only narrowly missing her eye as she batted her fists at its nose.

It lunged for her again, so close she could smell the rotting meat odor of its breath. The great wolf's weight pinned her to the carpet, crushing the air from her lungs.

And then it was gone.

Seth pulled the wolf back by the scruff of its neck and threw it against the wall with enough force to knock the animal unconscious. As soon as it hit the floor, it transformed again, becoming a wiry man with sandy, scruffy hair and a distinctive tattoo on his chest. Sera pushed herself to her feet and took a deep, shaky breath.

"Think he was here for you, or me?" Sera asked.

"I don't like either answer." Seth went to the open door, peering out into the darkness. He checked to the left and right before slamming it closed and engaging the locks. "We don't open that door again."

"What about the pizza?"

"Fine, *you* don't open that door again."

Sera kicked at the unconscious man's ankle. "What are we going to do with him? Call the cops?"

"No," Seth said quickly. "We don't want to do that."

"Why not? We didn't do anything wrong. This guy attacked us!"

"Yes, he did, but the police and the Brotherhood have a...complicated relationship."

"The cops are crooked?"

"Not all of them, but enough take bribes that they wouldn't be above placing a call to the Alpha."

"And tell him exactly where we are," Sera guessed.

"Precisely."

"Well, I don't want this asshole waking up in here. We've got to do something with him."

"I say we question him. We'll just need to make sure he can't go anywhere."

Seth stripped the bed as he spoke, yanking the blankets to the floor and pulling the sheets free from the mattress. He worked quickly, tearing the sheet into strips and then braiding three of the long pieces together to form a thick, hardy rope. Once Sera saw what he was doing, she began making a rope as well, and soon they had enough to bind his ankles, wrists, and throat.

Once they had him bound to the chair and positioned in the far corner, there was another knock on the door.

"I'll get this one," Seth announced.

"Wait." In all the excitement, Sera totally forgot that he was naked. She handed him a towel to wrap around his waist, which he took with a wink, and to her horror, a flush crawled up her throat and covered her cheeks. "I, uh...here's twenty bucks to give the guy."

Seth opened the door only wide enough to exchange the money for the pizza box, using his body to block the delivery boy's view of the room. A half-naked man in a motel room wasn't anything unusual, but a half-naked man with another man bound and gagged in his room might attract the wrong kind of questions.

"Good God, I'm starving," Seth announced, opening the box with a wild grin. It came with a little tub of parmesan cheese and chili flakes, and he covered the pizza with both before tearing into it. Sera merely watched as he downed the first three slices without pausing. "Shifting takes a lot of energy," he explained around a mouthful of the fourth slice.

"It would appear so. Mind if I get in on one of those slices?"

He passed the box to her with a sheepish grin. "It's good pizza."

Sera returned his smile and bit into a greasy,

cheesy slice. It *was* good pizza, but not quite as good as the view. Now that he was awake and moving, she had a completely different appreciation of his tall, lean body.

He moved with an unconscious grace, each gesture fluid and easy. It wasn't difficult to imagine him as a wolf, prowling through the shadows and the moonlight.

Sera chewed her pizza thoughtfully, her attention shifting to the strange man on the floor. The tattoo on his chest confirmed who sent him, but there were no other clues to his identity, no distinctive scars or other points of interest. As she studied him, his eyes began to flutter and he began to twitch.

"Shit! I think he's waking up!"

Seth crossed the room to their prisoner, grabbed him by a fistful of hair and slapped his face. Hard. Hard enough to pull him completely into the waking world.

As soon as his eyes opened, he began to struggle, but the makeshift ropes held strong and he wasn't able to escape. Seth slapped him again, drawing his attention, and they stared at each other in a silent, but obvious, power struggle.

The stranger was the first to look away, his shoulders slumping and his gaze shifting to the ground.

"What's your name?" Seth growled.

"Braxton."

"Who sent you?"

Braxton didn't answer. Seth still had a handful of the man's hair and he gave him a good shake, like a wolf might shake a pup.

"Who sent you?"

Braxton didn't seem afraid of Seth, but he still cast down his eyes and muttered, "The Brotherhood."

"Why?" Seth asked.

The question required another hard shake and a slap to the face before Braxton grudgingly said, "This bitch is making the Alpha nervous. She's showing Dwight's picture all over town, asking about some dead girl. He doesn't like it."

"Why not? Does he have something to hide?"

"Look, I don't know, man. Don't hit me again. I'm not even a full member of the pack, okay? He doesn't tell me anything. I just get my orders and try not to get killed."

"What's Dwight's last name?"

"I don't know. Jones? I don't even know the fucking guy. I saw him once."

"He has a scar?" Sera asked.

"Yeah, that's the guy."

Seth looked at her with an arched brow and a silent question-*do you believe him?* Sera nodded as a few more pieces of the puzzle fell into place. She'd been right. This Dwight was the key to understanding what happened to her sister and she was the only one who could excavate this particular cover-up.

Seth released his hair and crossed to Sera's side. "What do you want to do with him?"

"Can we just leave him here for the housekeepers to find in the morning?"

"Where are we gonna go?"

"I have a place. The rain is letting up; I think we can get there in one piece."

Seth nodded and returned to Braxton's side. He got the man's attention with another fistful of hair, leaning down to stand nose-to-nose with him. He inhaled deeply, his nostrils flaring as he marked Braxton's scent.

"The *bitch*, as you so charmingly called her, is a lot nicer than I am and she wants to let you live. But I suggest you leave Portland—hell, you may even want to get out of Oregon. Find yourself a new pack and have a healthy, long life. Because if I catch wind of you around town, I will tear your head off and dump your body in the woods. Do you understand me?"

Braxton nodded frantically. "I'll go, man, I'll go. I don't even like it here."

"Excellent." He turned his attention to Sera. "Ready?"

"Let's roll."

"Wait. Are you just going to leave me here?"

"They'll find you in the morning," Sera said, opening the door. The rain was still falling, but it was more of a sprinkle than a wall of water. "Besides, it'll give you plenty of time to think about your options."

"Pleasant dreams," Seth said as flicked off the light and closed the door behind him.

"Um...do you want to go get your clothes?"

"They've been lost. Torn to shreds when I shifted back in the woods."

"What about a wallet? Money? Anything?"

"I'll need you to spot me a few bucks, but I promise I'll pay you back."

Sera nodded. It would be worth twenty bucks to get him covered up. At least then she would be able to think about something other than how great he looked—and how much better he would look towering over her, positioned between her legs.

"Okay, we'll get some clothes, we'll get some sleep, and in the morning, we'll get to the bottom of the Brotherhood," Sera announced. It felt good to have a plan—or a jumping-off point, at least. Something more concrete than a picture of a stranger and a gut feeling.

Seth studied the photo of Aiza for a long, silent moment. Sera studied his face while he did so, looking for any flicker of recognition, any mild change of expression that would betray him. But there wasn't as much as a twitch of an eye. His face was as still as stone as he passed the picture back to her.

"I've never seen her before. Sorry; I never spent much time in Portland."

Sera shrugged. "It was worth a shot. It's just...what was she *doing* with those assholes? You know? What business did she have with them?"

"Was she a wolf?"

"No. I mean...I don't know. I hadn't seen her or heard from her in years. She could have been turned into one. But I thought that was generally frowned upon?"

Seth nodded in confirmation. "It is. And it's downright banned by the Brotherhood. They'll allow turned wolves in the pack, but if anybody is caught turning a werewolf, they're executed."

"Wow. Wait...*they're* executed?"

"Both the wolf and the one they're turning."

"Do you think that's what happened to Aiza?"

"I don't know."

"How can we find out?" Sera asked. "Is there a way to tell if Aiza was a wolf when she died? Would it have been in the coroner's report?"

"Unlikely."

"What about her medical records?"

"Only if she volunteered the information."

"There *has* to be a way. You've never needed to test to see if a body is also a werewolf?"

"It comes up less than you think." Seth folded his arms and ducked his chin, giving the impression of studying the ground; she could almost see the wheels turning behind his eyes. "There's a way. But we'd have to...do something you probably don't want to do."

"What? Tell me."

"Exhume her body."

"We'd have to dig her up?" Sera couldn't believe she was considering this, but knowing the answer could be the key to solving the mystery. "What then?"

"We expose her skin to wolfsbane."

"Wolfsbane?"

Seth smiled. "It's a flower. That'll be easy enough to get—it grows wild all over the place."

"Then I guess we'll just need some shovels."

Seth's smile transformed into a frown. "Are you sure about this? It'll be mighty hard to explain why we're digging up a body when the cops come."

"Then we better not get caught. We'll go to the store in the morning and get shovels and head torches and we'll dig a big hole."

He looked skeptical at that. "In the middle of the day?"

"No, tomorrow night. That'll be soon enough. In the meantime, maybe you should help me go through her room."

"You want me to help you go through your dead sister's personal belongings?"

"If you wouldn't mind." Sera took a deep breath, understanding her request was a little strange. "I think a second pair of eyes will help. Besides, there might be some Brotherhood or wolf-related information that I don't recognize, but you might."

"I'll be happy to help in any way I can, but I can't guarantee anything."

"It's better than no help at all."

Sera had been through every drawer and nook and cranny, but she'd left everything where she found it. Now she was glad she didn't quite have the heart to tuck her sister's life away completely. If there were any clues to be found, Sera didn't want to be guilty of disrupting the evidence.

They began to rummage, and minutes later, Seth straightened from his perusal of Aiza's bottom drawers. "Well, this might be something."

"What have you got?"

"A collar."

"A collar? Like, a dog collar?"

"Yes. An electric dog collar. With your sister's name on it."

"What? Let me see that. Why on earth...what would she have this for?" Sera physically recoiled at the thought of her sister wearing that thing, using it, being punished with it. "It's probably not just a sex thing, is it?"

"We won't know until after we do the wolfsbane test. But if I were a betting man, I'd say it probably wasn't a sex thing." At her inquiring look, he added, "A human that's turned into a werewolf lacks the instinct to shift from their wolf form to their human form, but a good shock to the system, like from this collar, will do the trick." He paused, tilting his head. His nostrils flared. "Stephanie is here."

"What? How do—" The chime of the doorbell halted her question. "Who's Stephanie?"

"She's the female alpha of my pack. I hope you don't mind, I called and gave her the address when we got here."

Sera shook off the pang of disappointment. Of course he'd call for a ride at the first opportunity. "As long as she wasn't followed, I don't mind. Hey, did you tell her how we met?"

"I told her you helped me get away from the Brotherhood. That's all she needs to know."

The doorbell chimed again and Seth hurried to the front of the house. Sera's attention shifted back to the collar, her active imagination easily conjuring a thousand scenarios linking Aiza's death to the darker implications of the electrified leather. She frowned, studying the leather closer. It was clearly hand stitched, made to order and personalized. Somebody poured effort and love into its creation.

"Sera? Do you mind coming out here for a minute?"

Sera stashed the collar in the drawer. "Coming." Maybe he wanted to say goodbye. Or maybe this Stephanie wanted to get a good look at her. Sera knew nothing about the hierarchy of wolf packs, and she wasn't sure if being the alpha female meant she was also involved in some way with Seth.

The first thing that struck Sera was the other woman's height—she was easily six feet tall, and she was not wearing heels. Her tall frame was well-muscled and nicely curved, and her almond-shaped eyes and pointed nose gave her a distinctively pretty face.

Her light brown hair was pulled back into a sloppy bun and she wore ratty gray sweatpants and an oversized sweater. A duffel bag sat on the floor at Seth's feet, and she was looking him over with thin-lipped concern and more than a hint of exasperation.

"Stephanie Tanner, this is Sera Simpson."

Stephanie's grip was firm but her smile was friendly as they shook hands, and it was clear her exasperation was reserved for Seth. "It's a pleasure to meet you," she said. "And thanks for helping this idiot avoid a broken neck."

"Um, well, it was the least I could do," Sera said, finding herself warming to the other woman.

"Yeah. Seth told me you've got your own unfinished business with the Brotherhood. Don't worry, he didn't go into any details, but you should avoid those guys if you can. I'm going to tell you the same thing I told him: go home. Where it's safe."

"Well, thanks for the warning, but I can't go anywhere. Not until I find out what they did to my sister."

Stephanie studied her for a moment and then offered an understanding nod. "I get it." She looked back to Seth. "I brought everything you asked for. Is there anything else I can do?"

Seth took one of the pictures of Dwight from his shirt pocket. "See what you can find out about this man. His name is Dwight and he may have been the last one to see Aiza alive."

"Brotherhood scum?"

"The sort you find at the bottom of a swamp, I'd imagine."

"On it. Any word on Tony or Chen?"

Seth shook his head with a grim frown. "Not yet, but the trail isn't cold."

"I'll call you when I know anything." She turned

to Sera, surprising her with a quick, tight hug. "We'll get to the bottom of this."

"Thank you."

"I'll walk you out," Seth said. He was outside with Stephanie for a long time—long enough that Sera had enough time to start cooking breakfast and drive herself crazy with all the images of what they might have been doing outside—but she played that off as he entered the kitchen. "I hope you like eggs."

"Even if I didn't, I'm starving. Can I do anything to help?"

"You can grate that cheese. I thought she was coming to pick you up."

"Did you want me to leave? I can call her."

"No," Sera answered quickly. "No, I...I'd like you to stay. But I thought maybe you'd want to go."

"I want to help you."

"And Stephanie? She wants to help me, too?"

"Let's just say you're not the only one who's lost someone to the Brotherhood. Now, let's figure out what we're going to need tonight—besides no rain and a lot of luck."

3

SERA HELPED SETH EXCAVATE THE DIRT, BUT WHEN IT came time to desecrate her sister's grave, she had to excuse herself. Seth nodded and helped boost her to the surface. She shined the flashlight down into the hole, turning her head as Seth broke the coffin open. He coughed with surprise as the smell of death and rot exploded from the broken latch. Sera kept her eyes averted until he shouted her name.

"What? What is it?"

"Lower the rope."

She dropped the end of the thick rope down and helped pull him out of the hole. "Well? What happened? Is she...?"

"Her skin definitely reacted. I think it's safe to say she'd been turned into a werewolf."

"And the Brotherhood killed her because of it?"

"Maybe. They've been known to kill for less. Look, why don't you head on home and I'll finish up here?"

"No, I can't leave you to deal with this by yourself."

"The sun will be up soon."

"All the more reason I should help."

"Really, I think it would be best if you went home," Seth said.

"Well, I think it'll be best for me to stay." She passed him the shovel. She needed time to process her emotions and she needed time to think. Since she couldn't go to her gym, she'd stay right there at the gravesite. "Let's get to work before somebody calls the cops."

They worked in silence only punctuated by the dull thud of dirt being returned to the grave. How long had her sister been living her life as a wolf? Had she told anybody about her secret? Had she lived, would she have confided in anybody? Sera felt strangely hurt that even this sort of metamorphosis hadn't prompted Aiza to pick up the phone.

They finished just as the approaching sun colored the sky flannel gray and pink. She let Seth drive them home, half asleep for the ride. She didn't remember getting home or how she made it from the car to the bedroom, but once she was under the covers, she fell into a deep, dreamless slumber. Her body was eager to catch up on all the sleep she'd lost since that first call from her parents, and nothing disturbed her for a solid twelve hours. When she finally woke again, it was to the smell of bacon and pancakes and the sounds of Seth knocking around in the kitchen.

He's still here? How is he still here?

Right on the heels of that surprise was another stunning revelation: she was actually very glad he hadn't left while she was zonked out. If they'd met under any other circumstances, she would have already made a move and asked him out on a date. Maybe under other circumstances, he would have accepted the invitation. He certainly seemed to like her.

Or maybe he saw her the same way she claimed to view him—as a means to an end. Nothing more or less than that.

Sera didn't realize how stiff she was from their grave-digging adventure until she stood and tried to stretch. Her shoulders pulled tight and her arms ached so much she could barely lift them over her head. She hadn't felt that exhausted and sore after a workout in years, and she had to admit, a part of her welcomed the pain. It meant she'd done hard work. It meant she was alive.

But it also meant she would kill for a good massage.

She shuffled into the kitchen, her pain forgotten when Seth smiled at her. "Good morning. Well, actually, good evening." He gestured at the stove. "I hoped your nose would wake you."

"Where did you get all this food?" Bacon, sausage, ham, eggs, pancakes, toast, oatmeal, cinnamon rolls, coffee, and orange juice waited for her.

"I had plenty of time to go shopping."

"Why is there so much?"

"After all that work and sleep, I thought you might be as hungry as I am," Seth explained as he poured the coffee.

"You thought right." Her stomach felt hollow, though she didn't really have an appetite. The food looked great but didn't appeal to her at all. Still, she accepted the heaping plate and the coffee, determined to finish off both. She needed the calories and the nutrients if she was going to see this through to the end.

Once she was done, Seth took the plate and

refilled her mug of coffee. "Stephanie called me earlier. She doesn't have any new information about our friend Dwight, but she found somebody who knew your sister."

Sera's eyes widened. "Who? What did they say?"

"Stephanie didn't go into the details, but if we want to talk to her, she said she's at the park every day, around noon."

"Weird. Why not just give you her number?"

"Apparently, she's willing to talk, but not over the phone, and she won't give her name."

"How did Stephanie find her?"

"Stephanie knows a *lot* of people and most of the wolves in the state." Seth downed a glass of orange juice before adding, "I'm not surprised she was able to track down a lead."

"She seems pretty cool. How long have you known her?" Sera asked, hoping she didn't sound too interested in the answer.

"She seems pretty cool because she *is* pretty cool. We've been pack mates all our lives. We worked our way up to alpha together and the pack has never been stronger."

"So, are there any little pups in the pack?"

"Sure, but none of them are ours." He met her

eyes and added, "Stephanie and I are not together, if that's what you're asking."

"I...no...that's not any of my business, is it?"

"It could be your business."

Sera's mouth felt dry. "How?"

"You could make it your business to know. Like this. Do you have a boyfriend?"

Sera shook her head.

"A lover? A suitor? Anybody who would mind if I did this?"

Seth took her hand and brought it up to his lips. She expected a courtly kiss, but instead he caressed her knuckles with his lips, his tongue darting out to trace her skin. It was brief but strangely obscene and undeniably sexy. Her throat tightened and all she could do was shake her head.

"So?" Seth prompted. "Make it your business, if that's what you want to do."

"Do you have a girlfriend? A lover?" She threaded her fingers through his and pulled his large hand to within kissing distance. She mimicked him, thrilled by the clean, salty taste of his skin. "Anybody who will mind if I do this?"

"No, not at all."

Sera didn't release his hand. She couldn't stop kissing the smooth skin. Nothing had ever felt so good against her lips, and she wanted more. She wanted to feel the velvety texture against her entire body, wanted to lose hours exploring the rich, silky planes of his body. He didn't seem to have a problem with that, as he did nothing to break contact with her questing mouth.

It'd only been a few months since Sera had sex, but it seemed like a lifetime since she'd been sensual with a man. Her desire was a slow burn, glowing a little hotter each time she got a taste of him.

She pulled his index finger between her teeth, gently biting the pad as she swirled her tongue over the tip. He watched her with hooded eyes and she couldn't resist smiling back. His fingers curled beneath her chin and he pulled her closer, tilting his head towards her. His finger slid from between her lips, freeing her mouth to be claimed by his.

But the kiss didn't come.

Instead, his ringing phone split the silence and drove them apart.

"Sorry." He snatched the phone up from the counter. "I've got to take this. It's Stephanie."

Sera nodded and stifled the flare of disappointment. Of course he had to take it. His pack mates were missing. Her sister was *dead*. They didn't have time to make out like teenagers in the kitchen.

"I'll be right there. Don't move." He put the phone in his pocket. "I'm sorry, I've got to go."

"What's wrong?" Sera asked.

"It's Chen. He was found wandering in the woods. The police have him now. I need to go and get him."

"I'll come with you," Sera said.

"No," Seth said sharply. He took a deep breath and softened his tone. "This is pack business."

Her first impulse was to argue her case, but she conceded with a small nod. He was right, of course. Just because she invited him into her personal matters didn't mean she had a right to tag along to his.

"You go take care of that. I've got some things to pack." She fled the room, and a moment later, she heard the front door open and close behind him.

4

Sera's car was back in the morning, but Seth was nowhere to be found. By noon, she felt a twinge of worry for him. What if the Brotherhood had tracked him down? It was hard to believe they'd attack him in broad daylight in the middle of Portland, but Sera had believed stranger things.

But when the sun sank and he hadn't returned, she was forced to admit that he probably wouldn't be returning. He'd only been in Portland to track down his pack mates, and now that they'd been found, he likely took them home.

Sera couldn't deny her disappointment. She never got his number and he was unlikely to have hers. When she wasn't thinking of Seth, her mind went to the man who'd tried to kill her only two nights before. She hadn't been afraid as long as Seth was there, but she hated being alone. Especially in a strange house, with a strange kitchen and a strange bed.

Not to mention the strange reminders of her sister's secret life.

She'd found a large, rawhide bone tucked under the bed, half of it gnawed away. This would be a perfectly normal thing to have in a home with a dog the size of a German Shepherd, but Aiza didn't have a dog.

There was another, smaller shock collar in the guest bedroom—or what Sera had assumed was the guest bedroom. As she went through the drawers and closet, it became clear that a man had lived there—or at least slept there regularly—but none of the clothes bore the sign of the Brotherhood or any other clue.

Looking for a distraction, she went to the kitchen and said a quick prayer of thanks for Seth's earlier trip to the grocery store. Sera grabbed the eggs, cheese and bacon, her mouth watering for an omelet, and the lights flashed out. A split second later, thunder boomed, close enough to rattle the windows and send Sera's heart to her throat, and the eggs fell forgotten from her fingers.

"Woo, okay, calm down. It's just thunder. No reason to be all jumpy." She took a deep breath, grabbed her phone for its light and left the kitchen, seeking the comfort of Aiza's plush couch and cozy afghan. She sank into the deep cushions and tried to tell herself that the rain was soothing and the lightning was just a free fireworks show, but her nerves were raw and a tension headache began to develop behind her eyes.

Just then, a loud crash that had nothing to do with thunder jarred her to her feet.

It came from the back of the house. It might have been the storm blowing over the garbage cans, but Sera wasn't taking any chances. She detoured to the kitchen for a knife and made her way to the back of the house.

"Who's out there?" she shouted over the fury of the storm. "I have a gun, asshole!"

"Don't shoot! It's just me."

"Seth? What are you doing here? Why are you slinking around the back?" She flung the door open. "Get in here, get in here."

"Sorry. I didn't mean to scare you." He slammed the door behind him and removed his hood; she was struck again by how gorgeous he was. Somehow, she'd forgotten just how unbelievable his cheekbones, strong nose, full lips and gray eyes were. "Do you really have a gun?"

She shook her head, showing him the knife.

"Well, maybe it wouldn't hurt to get you one."

"What? Why? What's going on? Was there somebody out there?"

"I didn't see anybody, but I think I caught the scent of two different wolves. Don't worry, if they come around again, they'll have to deal with *me*."

"What are you doing here?"

He frowned down at her. "Do you want me to go?"

"No, of course not. I thought...I didn't think you'd be coming back."

Seth tilted his head, still considering her. "I didn't think I'd be coming back, either. But once I got Chen home, all I could think about was getting back here to you."

"Do you...do you want to get out of those wet clothes?"

"Yeah. Yeah, I do."

She took him by the hand and led him down the hallway to the bedroom. He kicked the door shut behind him and Sera hesitated for a moment—until he took her other hand and guided it to his belt. She reacted automatically, pulling the leather strap free and popping the top button of his jeans.

After that, everything seemed so easy. She unzipped his pants and pushed them down while he toed off his boots. His shirt followed, and though it was almost completely dark in the room, she knew his body well enough to see every inch of him clearly.

Once his clothes were gone, he began undressing her. As soon as she felt the brush of his fingers against her skin, shivers went down her back and goosebumps erupted across her chest. The pads of his fingers were a little rough, but his blunt nails were as smooth as polished stone. Standing toe to toe, she realized just how tall he was, and she had to tilt her head back to angle her mouth for his kiss.

At first, his mouth was tentative. Almost shy. She parted her lips, inviting him to deepen the kiss, shuddering at the first brush of his tongue. She took a deep breath through her nose, inhaling the scent of his soap. Somehow, that seemed more intimate than the pressure of his mouth against hers and it drove home the fact that she was truly standing there, locked in his arms, yielding to his hard body.

And it felt right.

More than right.

It felt like coming home.

The thought wasn't exactly soothing. What if he left the next morning and didn't come back again? What if this was just a fling for him? Some sort of fun diversion?

But he touched her like he didn't want to stop, and so she decided to put her doubts aside and turn herself over to the overwhelming sensations of pleasure and desire rolling through her.

When he broke the kiss to catch his breath, she pulled him toward the bed. He followed her to the mattress, their mouths fusing together as they fell. He gripped her hips and rolled onto his back, settling her on top of him with a satisfied grunt.

She swiveled her hips, grinding against his stiff member. Heat flooded her, and her slick juices coated his length, preparing him for her tight entrance.

Their passionate kisses continued while they learned each other's bodies with yearning hands. He cupped her breasts against his palms, squeezing them with just enough pressure to make her moan, while her fingers sought out the lines of his chiseled muscles, looking for any tender point or spot of vulnerability.

She only moved away from his mouth because

she needed to taste his jaw and his throat; needed to lick the sweat from his Adam's apple.

"Are you ready?" he rasped.

Sera moaned, feeling as though she'd been born ready for this moment. She reached between their bodies, taking his shaft in her fist. His flesh pulsed against her palm, and his head was slick with his pre-cum. She stroked him slowly, her pussy clenching with anticipation with each slide of her hand. He moaned, his hips rising, seeking out more of her heat.

"God, Sera. I need to be inside of you."

She barely heard him beneath the buzzing in her eyes. Her mouth suddenly felt parched, and her fingers trembled where she touched him. With a deep breath, she shifted her hips and slid his head down to her entrance.

She braced herself against his chest and pushed back. His head breached her entrance, enough to make both of them gasp, but he slipped out. She reached for him again, gripping him tightly as she took in the head of his cock. With him securely positioned, she moved back, inch by slow inch, until he was fully sheathed.

In that moment, lightning flashed, illuminating

them and burning that moment into Sera's memory forever.

She didn't realize how much she truly wanted—truly *needed*—to feel him until he was buried inside of her. She arched her back, mouth open in silent amazement as their bodies found a natural tempo. The steady, unrelenting rhythm brought out something primitive inside of her. She clawed at him, bouncing faster and harder, surrendering completely to the primal, basic rhythm.

The storm picked up intensity, the wind howling like a mighty wolf, the rain beating relentlessly against the roof. The crashing thunder obscured her shouts of pleasure, each one tearing through her. She couldn't hear him over the chaos outside, but she felt his groans and grunts vibrating through his solid chest.

She leaned forward, pressing her chest to his, hungrily seeking out his mouth, burying her fingers in his hair, twining through the strands as their tongues dueled.

Seth's hands moved from her hips, sliding up her back and over her shoulders, then down her arms. His strong fingers locked around her wrists. Without breaking their tempo, he flipped them over, pinning her to the mattress. She arched beneath him, rising

up to meet his downward stroke, keening with pleasure as he impaled her.

Sera felt herself ascending to another level,
where there were only bliss and desire and needs
answered. For a moment, she was beyond the pain
and confusion of losing Aiza, the fear of being
hunted by a wolf pack, and even the loneliness she
thought she'd made peace with. Caught up in the
torrent of their shared passion, Sera forgot everything but the raw, electric heat of their bodies
joining.

Her scream at the moment of climax was muffled
by his mouth, and she unleashed the full force of her
orgasm against his rock-hard body. He shuddered,
pumping into her until they were both completely
spent.

It was a long time until either one of them could
speak.

"What happened?"

Seth sighed, revealing the depth of his exhaustion. "Can we talk about it in the morning?"

A part of Sera didn't want to talk about it at all.
She wished they could remain exactly like that,
blissed out and peaceful. "If you're going to be here
in the morning."

"I'm going to be here in the morning," Seth promised.

Sera buried her face against his chest, nuzzling in as close as she could. "I feel...good. For the first time in a long time."

"Me, too."

The regular beat of his heart lulled her to sleep, despite the persistent flashes of lightning. The storm faded from her awareness until she was lost in the darkness, warm and tired, past the point of dreaming.

It felt like she'd only visited this twilight land for a few seconds before a crashing boom shattered her peace and pulled her into a seated position. A second and third crash followed in rapid succession, and Sera knew it wasn't thunder.

"Get down," Seth whispered, pushing her back to the mattress. He shielded her body with his, his breath hot and rapid against her cheek.

"Are those gunshots?"

"Yes."

"Is somebody shooting at the house?"

"It sounds that way," Seth said grimly.

Panic pierced her like a dagger of ice. Would they just keep firing at the house? Or would they break in and try to finish the job?

"Where's my phone? I'm calling the cops."

"The cops aren't going to help," Seth whispered in the silence between shots. "They'll make sure they won't get here in time."

"Nobody will stop those maniacs from murdering us?"

"We're going to get out of here."

"How?" Sera asked.

"I'll be the distraction. You just focus on getting to the car."

"And leaving you here to be shot?" Sera shook her head. "No. No way. Nope."

"I'll be right behind you."

"I'm not going to leave you to get shot."

"Okay, get under the bed. Don't move until I come and get you."

"What the hell are you going to *do*?" Sera demanded.

But he was already gone. She slid off the bed and under the mattress, praying that he didn't get his fool head shot off. "Not now, Lord. Not when I've just barely found him."

She didn't know him well enough to say she was in love with him, but the thought of never seeing his bright gray eyes again made her stomach roll and heave.

An eternity passed while she waited. The gunshots grew sporadic and then stopped altogether. "Please be a good sign. Oh please."

The bedroom door slammed open and from her perspective, she could see Seth's bare feet. She sighed with relief and began to shimmy from beneath the bed. Her relief was quickly replaced by terror as the lightning revealed his statuesque body covered in dark splashes of blood.

"S—Seth?"

"Run."

"What?"

"Run!" he roared as his body morphed into a long, lean wolf. The shout turned into a howl, his eyes twin discs of silver, his long, wicked teeth descending from his massive snout. Sera forced her numb legs to work, running past the wolf and into the night's angry maelstrom.

5

SETH RAN HOT ON SERA'S HEELS. SHE HEARD HIM growling and barking through the downpour, but she didn't look down, didn't let anything distract her from the goal of reaching the car. She'd grabbed her purse as she fled the house, and she had her keys in her hand before she reached the lock. As soon as she flung the door open, Seth jumped inside, soaking the seat with his giant muddy paws. Sera barely noticed. He was still growling at unseen assailants, and Sera couldn't tell if they were still firing shots or if the constant, teeth-rattling explosions were just booms of thunder. She had no intention of sticking around long enough to find out.

The engine roared to life and she threw the gearshift into drive and stomped on the accelerator.

The tires spun for a moment, unable to get any traction against the slick pavement, and then they lurched forward. It wasn't easy to stabilize the wheel as she careened into the street, but she got it under control by the end of the block.

"Do you want me to drive?" Seth asked from the passenger's seat. She was never going to get used to how quickly he could shift from man to wolf and back again.

"No, I've got it. Are you hurt?"

"I'm alright. This isn't my blood."

"How many of them were there?"

"It was hard to tell. I took out two and I could hear at least two more. Maybe three."

"Do you think they're following us?"

Seth turned his head and peered through the darkness behind them. "I don't see anything, but we're getting the hell out of Portland."

"Where are we going?"

"Yakima."

Sera frowned, rolling to stop at a red light. "Washington? What's there?"

"My pack. The Wolf Brotherhood is territorial. They're unlikely to follow us once we're out of their area." He checked over his shoulder once more, but their tail was still clear.

"I can't go with you to Yakima. I have stuff to do here. You know, like selling Aiza's house, solving her murder; important things."

"They *are* important things," Seth agreed, "but you're not going to be able to do anything if you're dead. The attack tonight...it was just a warning. Next time, they'll shoot to kill."

Sera swallowed hard. He did have a point. She wasn't going to be any help to Aiza if she was shot and buried in a shallow grave. But running all the way to Yakima? That might put her out of the reach of the Brotherhood, but it also put her investigation at a distinct disadvantage.

"Pull over at this gas station," Seth instructed.

"No. You're naked and covered in blood. If anybody sees you, they'll call the cops. Do you feel like trying to evade the police tonight?" Sera asked.

"Not particularly, no. But you don't know where we're going."

"Well, tell me."

"Get on I-5 North. We'll stop after we clear the city."

Sera nodded her head in agreement. Her heart was only now returning to its normal rate, and her breathing had almost normalized as well. She'd never been shot at before, and now that she had time to really think about how close she'd been to death, her hands shook. She ignored the trembling for as long as she could, focusing on navigating her way through the rain and traffic, but the shaking didn't stop. If anything, it grew more intense, sending mini-earthquakes through her limbs until her teeth were chattering.

Seth leaned over and a placed a steadying hand on her shoulder. The heat and strength she felt in his grip did provide a modicum of comfort, but she'd never been so close to her own death. It was difficult enough to wrap her mind around her sister's mortality—coming face to face with her own in such a sudden, violent way was almost too much to deal with.

"We're going to get to the bottom of this," Seth promised in a low, urgent voice.

"I know."

"And I'm not going to let anything happen to you."

"I appreciate that."

They drove in silence until Sera exited the freeway for a mostly empty truck stop. The gas station had some T-shirts and golf shorts, and she grabbed a change of clothes for each of them, as well as plenty of salty and sweet comfort food, water, and a case of beer she intended to crack into at the first opportunity. When Seth emerged from the bathroom in his tourist clothes, he should have looked silly, but instead he made Sera forget everything as her mouth watered for him.

The T-shirt was at least a size too small and it hugged every chiseled line of his rock-hard abs. The shorts showed off most of his legs, and even though he went into that bathroom naked, it was as if she'd never seen him before.

Is this how it'll always be? Will I always be surprised by the sight of him? It seemed more than likely, as now she knew he felt and tasted as good as he looked.

"I'll drive."

Sera handed him the keys and crawled into the back seat. She didn't think she'd be able to sleep, but she appreciated the chance to lie down.

"How far?"

"A little over two hundred miles. It'll go by quickly, especially if you can take a nap," Seth promised.

He turned on the classic rock station, and Sera stretched out in the backseat, the songs carrying her mind to Aiza and the long summers they spent in the backseat of their father's Chevy, sometimes reading or coloring in compatible silence. Sometimes that silence would erupt in outbursts of shouting or even violence—they'd both resorted to hair pulling if necessary—and then their father would threaten to pull over and give them both a spanking they'd never forget. Such a warning would be enough to calm Sera, but Aiza never knew fear.

The road lulled her to sleep, but the memories didn't stop. They just rolled into dreams. Dreams of a dark-haired girl who stared at the moon with a look of unbelievable longing. *Wouldn't it be great if we could run? If we could run with the moon?*

"Sera, sweetheart, wake up. We're here."

Here was a squat cabin surrounded by trees near a river. She could hear the running water, but she couldn't see it through the darkness. He took her by the arm, guiding her over the stone path and to the front door. They stepped into a cool room, the interior as modern as the exterior was rustic.

"Lights. Low." The room was flooded with a warm light as soon as he spoke, revealing a plush leather couch and recliner, rich hardwood floors, a fireplace with a marble mantel and dark mahogany tables. The television was large, but not excessively so, and his movie collection lined one wall while his books dominated the other. It was cozy. Sera could see herself getting quite comfortable there.

"Have a seat," Seth said, gesturing at the couch. "I'll make some coffee and then I'll get you caught up."

Sera nodded, still groggy, and stiff from lying in the same position for too long. She curled up in the corner of the sofa, resting her head on the back and dozing off until a gentle hand nudged her awake.

"Maybe we should talk tomorrow," Seth said, passing her a steaming mug of perfectly prepared coffee, just the way she took it. "You still look as tired as I feel."

"What about your pack mates. Are they okay?"

"Chen will be fine. Tony..."

"What about Tony?"

"We don't know where he is," Seth stated grimly.

"Did Chen escape without him?"

"Escape?" Seth shook his head. "He doesn't remember being caught. He said he woke up in the woods and figured he must have been mugged. He claims he has no memory of what happened to Tony or who attacked them. The police have no physical evidence that there was an attack."

"So...what happened?"

"Nobody knows. I went to where they found

Chen to try to pick up Tony's trail, but he'd been wandering around for a couple of hours at least. Maybe even a couple of days. There wasn't any trail to follow."

"Well, we have to go back to Portland."

"No."

"What do you mean, no? If Chen was there, Tony is probably still there. He could be hurt. We have to find him."

"Of course. *I* will go find him. You will stay here."

Sera blinked at him. "What does that mean? Are you kidnapping me?"

"I'm protecting you. The Brotherhood won't follow us this far into Washington. I'll search for Tony and box up the rest of your sister's house."

"I can't just *not* go back to Portland."

Seth stared at her with a look of disbelief. "They shot at you. Repeatedly. Isn't that enough of a hint for you?"

"What am I supposed to do?" Sera demanded. "Let my sister's murder go unsolved?"

"Sera, I know this isn't easy for you. I know you want there to be an answer, something that makes this tragedy make sense. But maybe it was just an accident."

"Now you sound like them," Sera said coldly.

"What about everything we know? Hell, would the Brotherhood be trying to *kill me* if it truly was just an accident and they have nothing to hide?"

"Okay, say you're right and they've implicated themselves by targeting you. Are you willing to go to the cops with that information right now?" Seth asked.

"Absolutely."

"Why do you want to paint a target on your back?"

"Because they can't just get away with this!" Sera exploded, finally fed up with the whole conversation. She'd buried her sister *twice* now. She wasn't about to bury her a third time by dishonoring her memory. "They can't murder a woman and just get away with it. How is that...how can you live in a world like that?"

"I can live in a world where crimes go unsolved. It's terrible. It's brutal. But it's the world we've always lived in." Seth took her hand, his thumb moving over her knuckles. "What I can't do is live in a world where you are dead. If keeping you alive means you hate me, I can live with that, too."

Sera sat, stunned into silence. She didn't doubt his sincerity. She also didn't want to argue with him anymore. But she felt broken, sick in her heart. He took the seat beside her, wrapping his arms around her shoulders and pulling her against him. She melted into the embrace, thankful for his warmth and the solid reality of his body.

"BESIDES, I'm not going to give up." Seth promised. "I'll keep looking for clues while I pack up the house. And I'll follow up with that woman who agreed to speak with us. I'd just prefer if you stayed out of harm's way."

"So, you're asking me to stay here?"

"Yes."

"Why not just send me on home?"

"I'd like to get to know you better. If you don't mind staying..."

Sera couldn't imagine herself leaving. In that moment, she tried to picture returning to her call-center job, her single-serving life, her bleak apartment, and she just couldn't do it. She didn't even feel a twinge of desire to—how could she when his arms felt like home?

"Where will I be sleeping?"

"Allow me to show you." Seth stood without warning, sweeping Sera up into his arms. She laughed with surprised delight, her arms wrapped around his neck as he carried her through the living room and up a short flight of stairs.

The cabin's bedroom was a loft over the living space. A massive four-post oak bed dominated the center of the room and it looked so soft and inviting, all she wanted to do was sink into it for the rest of her life. He lowered her to the plush mattress and smiled as she stretched and rolled over the soft faux-fur blanket, suddenly feeling too constricted by the gas-station wardrobe.

"Help me get this off," she said, tugging at her T-shirt. He gently slapped her hands away and yanked the material over her head, pulling it hard enough to rip. He tossed it aside without a second glance and pulled her shorts off. He moved like he couldn't wait to get her naked again, and the heat from his gaze made her flush pink from head to toe.

He made short work of his clothes and then he was there, between her legs once again, his heavy-lidded eyes turning her insides to goo. She opened up to him, hooking her feet over his hips and pulling him in close. He positioned himself at her opening and slid into her without another word, filling her with a slow thrust. She caught her breath, almost unable to process the sudden difference in her world. Her flesh burned and stretched around the intrusion, her nerve-endings already singing for more.

Sera twitched and trembled, cupping the back of his head and dragging his mouth down to hers. Once their tongues touched, he started to move, rolling his hips against her. Her hands moved down his back, nails dragging against his skin as she clutched at him, pulling him closer, holding him tighter. She kissed him until she had to break away for air, and the musty scent of their coupling filled her head, making her dizzy.

His body was still so new to hers, and she was so sensitive to his touch, that it didn't take long until she was shuddering with pleasure. That didn't stop him, though. He shifted his angle, thrust into her with his determined strength, and a scream tore from her throat. Another followed, and another. He smashed his mouth to hers, muffling the sound as they flew over the final edge together.

6

Seth's cabin was beautiful, and he told her to make herself at home, indicating that nothing was off-limits while he was away. She was welcome to explore the rooms, his book and DVD collection, cook anything she wanted in his well-stocked and fully modern kitchen, or even go for a walk as long as she remained on his property. It was all very generous, and of course she was happy to be with him and glad to be protected from the Brotherhood, but she still felt like a bird in a cage. Perhaps a gilded cage, but a cage all the same. She knew that she wasn't his prisoner, and yet, she was his captive, willing though she may be.

Sera had nothing to distract her from her thoughts of Aiza. At least when she had the task of packing and cleaning the house, she had something to focus on. Also, her time was running low. She had a life, a job, and a house to get back to. A friend of hers was watering the plants and feeding the fish, but she couldn't remain on vacation indefinitely. Despite her restlessness and sadness, she found she wasn't actually looking forward to going home. She placed her calls and delayed her return home for another week, giving herself two more weeks with Seth.

Her days might have been boring, but her nights were full of passion. It was like Seth couldn't get enough of her, and she certainly hadn't had her fill of him. Every touch ignited her senses, every kiss made her hungry for a thousand more. When she lost herself in his arms, it was hard to remember that the rest of the world existed. Hard to remember there was anything but the sense of satisfaction and safety and pleasure that he gave her.

Stephanie arrived on the seventh day of her stay at the cabin, bringing a much-needed break to the monotony of her time there. She also brought two big sandwiches, beer, and an update on their hunt for Aiza's killer.

"You must be going crazy here all by yourself,"

Stephanie said, cracking open a can. She held it out
but snatched it back as Sera reached for it.

"What?"

Stephanie studied her with a frown. "Your scent
is...off."

"Off?" Sera flushed to scarlet. "Um, what do you
mean by that? I *did* shower this morning—"

"No, nothing like that. It's just...not the same."

Stephanie slowly handed the beer over, but Sera
had lost her taste for it. She'd lost her appetite, too.
"Not the same as what? The night we met?" When
Stephanie didn't answer, Sera pressed. "What do you
think it is?"

"It's probably too early to tell but..."

"But what?"

"I think you might be pregnant."

Sera blinked at her. Then blinked again. Pregnant? It was possible. She certainly hadn't insisted
on protection every time they had sex. But pregnant?
Now was not a good time to have a child. Maybe in a
year or two. If she and Seth were still together, she
would love to have a baby with him. But now? She
didn't even know how she felt about him and she
definitely didn't know what he felt for her. What if
he didn't want to spend his life tied to her?

"I'm sorry. I didn't want to freak you out,"

Stephanie said. "I shouldn't have said anything. I could be wrong."

"Do you...do you really think you could be wrong?"

Stephanie shook her head, still wearing a solemn frown. "Here. Eat your sandwich."

"Thanks," Sera muttered, though she still didn't have an appetite. She didn't taste it. Barely felt herself chewing it. *Pregnant.* She would take a test to confirm it, but deep down inside she knew the truth. She knew Stephanie was probably right. Sera took another bite of her sandwich because it was something to do, and Stephanie mirrored her. They chewed in silence, both caught up in their own thoughts.

"How am I going to tell Seth?" Sera finally asked.

"If it makes you feel better, you don't have to tell him."

"He'll be able to smell it?"

"He will," Stephanie confirmed. "If he hasn't already."

Sera shook her head. "I've only known him for two weeks."

"Maybe that's all you need if it's the right person."

"You think I'm the right person for Seth?" Sera

would never admit it out loud, but she did want Stephanie's approval, if only because she was so important in Seth's life.

Stephanie took her time to answer, chewing another bite of her sandwich and taking a deep drink before saying, "Yes."

"Care to expand on that? You don't even know me. How could you know I'm the right person for him?"

"You're right, I don't know you at all. But I know *him*. We grew up together. We've led the pack together for the past ten years. He's never been like this with anybody."

"Like what?" Sera asked.

"We lead the pack together because we took over when we were very young. Only eighteen. Since then, his only concern has been the pack. Taking care of his wolves. He's never dated anybody. He might have had some one-night stands, but nobody who stuck around long enough for breakfast. And you...he's moved you into his house."

"Well, the Wolf Brotherhood did try to kill us."

"Honey, don't take this the wrong way, but you have your own home and he has his own problems. He could have sent you home and walked away from the whole situation. Instead, he's brought your problems right into the middle of his life."

"Do you think it's too early for a test?" Sera asked.

"It might be, but I can pick one up at the drug store and you could take it anyway. I'll look for one that can give the earliest results."

"Where is he? He was gone this morning when I woke up."

"He's with Chen and a few other pack mates. Chen has been having a difficult time adjusting and there are some...concerns."

Sera had the feeling that she wasn't supposed to pry into Chen's issues or what those concerns might be. That was still pack business, and she wasn't part of the pack. For the first time in her life, it struck her that she wasn't a part of any pack or community. Her family was distant—so distant that they only spent a single day together in the wake of a tragic death. And her work was just that—work. She didn't socialize after hours and didn't care to make any connections with her co-workers. Her favorite pastimes were all solitary activities—reading, crafting, or taking long, quiet walks through her city's parks. She'd been alone for so long, it never occurred to her that there was any other way to be.

Now she had the opportunity to be a part of *something*. Her child would be born into a family. She'd already had a small taste of what that life would be like. Stephanie didn't even know her, and yet she'd been willing to search for leads and provide any other support she could. Seth had come back for her, and as Stephanie pointed out, made her problems his problems. Lightening her burden by sharing the load. A part of her was curious, excited by this sudden change of expectations.

And another part of her wanted to get away as quickly as she could.

Deep down inside, she knew the truth and feared that truth would become evident to everybody sooner or later. She had no business being in a pack. She didn't know the proper behavior of a pack mate, didn't know the dynamics of a healthy, functioning family. She wasn't even a wolf. Stephanie had been kind to her, but would the rest of his pack accept her?

"Hey." Stephanie put her hand on Sera's arm, dragging her attention back to the present. "Are you okay?"

"I...I don't know. There's so much to think about."

"I'll go get the test." Stephanie stood and gathered her purse. "Is there anything else you need?"

"Thank you, no. I don't think so. Nothing else I can think of right now, anyway."

Stephanie gave her arm a friendly squeeze and gathered up her purse. She promised to return soon, and then she was gone, leaving Sera alone with her own thoughts. For the first time in days, those thoughts weren't full of Aiza. But her sister hovered right on the periphery, a ghostly reminder that Sera would never have the pleasure of introducing her baby to his or her aunt.

My baby, Sera thought, her hand going to her soft stomach. Soon it would grow and swell, and she would feel the life they created. Would it be a wolf? Sera didn't know how that worked, but Seth probably would. What if her baby *was* a wolf? How would she raise it? How would she know what to do?

Her stomach growled then, so loud that it sounded like she might have a wolf in there after all. She still didn't have much of an appetite, but a different instinct guided her now. She didn't just need the energy for herself any longer; she needed it for her baby, so she could nurture its body, its organs, its tiny hands and feet. She scarfed down the giant sandwich, feeling a little better, a little stronger, with each bite.

Forty-five minutes after Stephanie left, she

returned with the test in hand and an apology. "I'm sorry it took so long. Something came up. I got a phone call." She handed the test over and added, "I've already called Seth."

"Called Seth. About what? The test?" The thought of him coming home now when she didn't even know the answer yet, much less what the hell she was going to say, nearly tipped her right over into panic.

"No. That phone call I got? That was from Amelia."

"Who?"

"The chick who said she'd meet you in the park to talk, but you guys never actually made it."

Sera nodded. "Oh right. What's going on? What did she say?"

"It sounds like Dwight has gone to ground and she has the address for his safe house," Stephanie said.

"How did she get that? Is she a reliable source?"

"Let's just say that he's a man of particular tastes and she is a good source." Stephanie guided Sera towards the bathroom. "Seth will be here soon."

Sera nodded. She definitely wanted to get this question answered. The sooner she could discuss it with Seth, the better. They needed to be on the same page as soon as possible. The stakes were too high to be left with any ambiguity. If he didn't want this baby, if he didn't want *her*, she would have to know so she could make her plans. She didn't even know where to begin.

Feeling herself begin to panic again, she took a deep breath and marched into the bathroom. One thing at a time. That was all she could do. Focus on one thing at a time and everything would be fine.

7

It was the strange, the difference between thinking you know something and *actually knowing* something. The heavy feeling in the pit of her stomach moved to her throat, tightening her vocal cords and holding her jaw closed. The more she wanted to say something, the more difficult it became to find the words. A part of her thought she could wait it out. Surely Seth would notice the difference in her scent, sooner or later. Surely, he would be forced to comment on that change. Eventually.

She was distracted and quiet during their meal, and so was he. The reality of the pregnancy crashed through her head like a hurricane, and she didn't quite register Seth's withdrawal. They watched a movie together after dinner, a quiet, normal activity, with her tucked safely in his arms. For the first time since Stephanie's visit, her raw nerves were soothed and she almost felt at peace.

They didn't make love, but he held her close in the dark. She listened to the steady rhythm of his breathing, tracking time with every exhale. She couldn't tell if he was sleeping or if he was still lost in his own thoughts, still consumed by his pack. She would ask him, but she still had the sense that his pack and his life were none of her business, though *her* life and her family seemed to be very much their shared business.

Her business was his business. *He's brought your problems right into the middle of his life.* That's what Stephanie had said. And this wasn't her problem alone; the baby was his, too.

For the first time, she felt her throat muscles relax and finally the words came. "I'm pregnant."

His hand moved immediately, as if by instinct, to her stomach and his arm tightened around her. "I know."

He held her so tightly she felt the press of his heartbeat against her back. Only then did she realize how tensely she was holding herself and she exhaled, forcing herself to unclench her muscles. In response, he held her closer, and she exhaled again, willing the stress to flow away.

"That's better," he murmured, his mouth close to her ear. The warmth of his breath made her shiver with pleasure, and more knots released from her stressed muscles. "Just keep breathing."

"I'm scared," she whispered.

"I know. But you don't have to be. I'm not going to let anything happen to you."

"We barely know each other." She couldn't speak above a whisper. She felt breathless.

"I know you're the one I want. I know I'll do anything necessary to keep you safe. And I know you don't have to make any decisions right now. Right now, all you have to do is let me hold you and get some sleep."

Tears stung the corners of her eyes, but she wasn't sad. She was relieved. The pain that had at her tense and afraid finally snapped free, allowing her to take a deep, completely unhindered breath.

"Stephanie said she had information about Dwight Lance...I haven't been able to think straight all day."

"She told me what she knew."

"Is there any good news?" Sera asked.

"I think we should talk after you rest."

"I won't be able to sleep if I don't know," Sera countered, though her eyes stung and her head felt heavy.

"We think we have a location. The safe house where he's hiding low. I need to check it out."

"What if it's a trap?"

"That's why I'm going to check it out before we do anything."

For the first time, Sera thought about the implications of that. She'd been interested in answers, an explanation, something that could give her a sense of closure, or at least of understanding. But now she realized she couldn't just walk up to the man and demand an explanation. It was far more likely he'd rip her throat out before she could get a single word out.

"Once you check it out, what are we going to do?" Sera asked.

"We'll save that discussion for later. You said you wanted to know what I know, and I told you." He kissed her temple. "Now go to sleep."

She closed her eyes and felt the last of her tension melt away as she drifted into sleep.

8

SERA HAD A VERY BAD FEELING.

Like she left the oven on in her apartment. Like her parents were trying to reach her but couldn't find her. Like there was an emergency and the phones were down, the roads were blocked, and a storm was closing in. She paced through Seth's house, unconsciously holding her abdomen while she looked for something to distract her from her growing sense of unease.

"You're just nervous because Seth isn't home. Calm down. He can't be with you all the time," Sera muttered, trying to talk some sense into herself before she had a nervous breakdown.

But it didn't *feel* like an unreasonable anxiety. It didn't feel like she was just being crazy and lonely.

She never claimed to be psychic or even have an uncanny sixth sense, but there was something wrong and she *knew* it. Seth had gone to scout Dwight's safe house, promising he would keep in touch and he would not take any unreasonable risks, but after his initial text telling her he'd arrived, there'd been radio silence.

After six hours of no news and no response to her texts, she couldn't take it anymore. She called Stephanie, her fingers shaking, her voice trembling.

"Have you heard from Seth?" she asked by way of greeting.

"No. Have you?"

"No. I think there's something wrong."

"I'll be there in ten minutes," Stephanie promised.

Sera paced through the cabin as she waited, her imagination unhelpfully supplying bloody scenario after scenario. In each one, Dwight was faster, stronger, meaner, deadlier, and Seth didn't have a chance. Considering how close he'd come to killing Seth already, and considering that he'd likely murdered Aiza, Sera found very little to comfort herself with. What reassurances did she have that he would be okay? What wellspring of hope could she draw on to sustain herself and their child?

"Do you know where he is?" Sera demanded as soon as Stephanie arrived. "He wouldn't tell me the exact location, but I figure you must have it."

"I have it. But he made it very clear that we were not to follow him."

"He should be home by now. He hasn't texted. He hasn't called. It's been *six hours*; we're not waiting here any longer," Sera announced.

"He forbade it."

"*Forbade?* Are you kidding me? I know he's the alpha but so are you! What if he needs us, Stephanie? What if he's waiting for us right now?" *What if he's already dead?* Sera forced that question out of her mind. She wasn't going to think like that. She couldn't. Not if she wanted to keep her wits about her.

"It's dangerous. This Dwight guy is very dangerous."

"So are you. Hell, so am I. Let's show that jerk what happens when he messes with a couple of dangerous bitches, yeah?"

Stephanie hesitated and for a moment, Sera thought she would have to do this alone. But then her thoughtful frown disappeared and she nodded in agreement. "Let's go get him. And then we'll wring the bastard's neck."

"You hold him down, I'll do the neck-wringing," Sera said.

"Deal."

There was an awkward silence as they both realized they had absolutely no idea how to stage a rescue mission. "So...what do we need?" Sera asked.

"A way to get in."

Sera nodded. "Weapons for once we get in."

"Weapons?"

"Well, you don't need one, but I do. A gun or a knife or something."

"I don't have a gun. Seth has some really sharp kitchen knives," Stephanie said.

"Okay, I'll grab one of those. You go get the car."

Stephanie nodded and then they were both in motion, and Sera realized they were actually going to do this insane, dangerous thing. She wasn't ignorant of the danger. Aiza had already lost her life and Seth's could very well hang in the balance. Could be hanging by a very thread. Her child would never know her aunt, but Sera would be damned if she allowed the same fate to befall Seth.

"Have you tried calling Seth again?" Stephanie asked as Sera slid into the passenger seat.

"Called and texted. No response."

"I tried, too." Stephanie put the car into gear with

a look of such grim determination, Sera almost laughed. Not because it was funny, but because she felt the same way on the inside.

"Tell me what you know about the place."

"It's a lake house just on the other side of the border. Just on the edge of the Brotherhood territory. My source didn't mention if there were guards, but Seth and I both think there's likely a few patrolling the property. She said it's not big. There's only one floor with two exits."

"So there's a back door and a front door. I guess we'll go in through the back door."

"It might be better to use the front. The back door opens into the kitchen and that's where my source always made her food deliveries. She said he was always waiting for her in there, watching TV and smoking."

"Then the front door. Or maybe a window?"

"Do you think Dwight would recognize you if he saw you?" Stephanie asked.

"Probably? He might have taken a good luck at me at the funeral."

"The funeral?"

"Aiza's funeral."

Stephanie looked at her from the corner of her eye. "He was there?"

"Yes."

"Why would he go to the funeral if he—if he had something to do with it?"

"I don't know. Maybe that's how he gets off."

"Well, maybe if we get a hat and some glasses he won't recognize you. You can knock on the kitchen door."

"And pretend to be his food delivery?"

"Precisely."

A plan began to form and Sera quickly opened up her notepad to make a list of what they would need. Mainly because it gave her an excuse to stare at her phone as she prayed for Seth to text her and put an end to their wild scheme. But the miles fell away and the minutes wore on—and a text did not come.

They made only one brief stop, to gather the supplies, and reached the cabin in just over an hour. Stephanie pulled off the road and parked in the woods about a half-mile from Dwight's driveway and killed the engine. "I think you should stay here while I do some recon. Maybe I can pick up Seth's scent or find his car."

"Be careful."

Stephanie nodded and began to undress. Sera averted her eyes while Stephanie disrobed and shifted, turning into a sleek, golden wolf. Sera reached over without thinking, her fingers seeking the thick, soft fur. Stephanie whined and pawed at the door, prompting Sera to lean over and push it open. The wolf disappeared into the trees, swallowed by the shadows.

Sera didn't waste a second. She put together the decoy box and slipped on an apron she lifted from the grocery store. She wasn't sure if that's what a delivery girl normally wore, but she thought it lent the entire enterprise an air of authenticity. And certainly, every little bit of authenticity could only help.

Her attention returned to the phone again and again, afraid she would miss a call from Seth or a text from Stephanie. Each second felt like a minute and every minute like an hour while she waited for Stephanie's return, her nerves multiplying on themselves until she thought she would scream, and still, there was no sign of either wolf.

A sudden knock on the window made her nearly jump from her skin, and it was so dark outside she couldn't tell right away that it wasn't Stephanie trying to get her attention. The second she unlocked the door, it was ripped open and a strong hand grabbed her by the shoulder and hauled her from the seat.

"What are you doing here?" Seth demanded in a furious whisper.

"I...I'm looking for you. Where have you been?"

"I've been in the top of a tree, scoping out the asshole. What are *you* doing?"

"I...you never replied or sent me a text or anything."

He looked over her shoulder. "This is Stephanie's car. Where is she?"

Sera nodded towards the shadows. "She went that way. She said she'd be right back."

Seth closed his eyes and took a deep breath. He caught the scent he was looking for and his whole body turned in that direction. "Stay here. I'm going to get her and we're going to get the hell out of here."

"I'm sorry, I didn't mean—"

"Just stay here. Get in the car. Don't unlock the door for anyone but me."

She nodded numbly and slipped into the car, locking the door as instructed. She was relieved to see him yet felt sick with guilt and worry. She'd panicked and potentially put them all at risk. It felt like the right thing to do at the time, but maybe that was why the road to hell was paved with good intentions. She unconsciously held her stomach, worrying her bottom lip with her teeth until she tasted a hint of copper.

It felt like an eternity passed before Seth and Stephanie returned, both of them running on two legs. Sera unlocked the doors just as they reached for the handles, and Seth dove behind the wheel, keys already in hand. He peeled out without a word, his jaw clenched, his eyes narrow as he navigated his way along the dark, winding road.

"I don't think anyone saw us," he checked the rearview mirror as he spoke, "but we may have tripped a motion sensor."

"Motion sensor?"

"Yeah, he's got motion sensors, silent alarms, cameras, floodlights. And guards. Lots of guards. All of them wolves. About what I expected."

But nothing like Sera expected. She'd actually thought they would be able to drive right up to the cabin and walk right up to the front door. She opened her mouth, but was unable to find her voice. She wanted to apologize, to explain, to try to make him understand that she was only doing what she thought was right. Only doing what she had to do to keep him safe.

Stephanie remained silent in the backseat.

Perhaps she was feeling the same shame over taking a foolhardy risk.

"There was something I wasn't expecting, though." Seth looked at her from the corner of his eye. "I saw Dwight. He wasn't alone in there."

"Who was he with?"

"Aiza."

"What? *What?* What are you talking about? Did you just say you saw him with my sister?"

"I saw Aiza with him," Seth confirmed.

"YOU SAW somebody who *looked* like Aiza. We...we *dug* up her body, Seth. How could she be in that cabin?"

"We dug up *a* body," Seth corrected grimly. "It wasn't her."

"You saw somebody that looks like her," Sera said again, feeling faint. How could that possibly true? How could her sister have faked her own death? Why would she go to such great lengths? And even if she had the perfect reason, how could this possibly be true? Confusion and anger hit her in matching waves and then fell away as she realized she could see her sister again. She could touch her and embrace her and tell her that she loved her still, had never stopped loving her.

"We have to go back."

Seth shook his head. "No, we don't want to do that."

"We have to! If she's there, like you said, we *have* to go back. I have to see her."

"Sera, you don't understand. She doesn't want to be found out."

"*He* doesn't want to be found out. She's probably his prisoner. She's probably waiting for somebody to figure it out and come for her. We can't just leave her there."

"Sera, listen—"

The sudden flood of bright headlights filled the car and cut off whatever Seth wanted to say. He pressed on the accelerator, but the truck behind them sped up as well.

"What the—"

Stephanie screamed and a second later, the truck slammed into the rear of the car. Seth fought to keep control, but the truck hit them a second time and sent them flying off the side of the road. Everything went bright—brighter than the sun—and then everything was black.

9

SERA CAME TO SLOWLY, HER HEAD SPINNING AS SHE tried to focus. Gradually, the blobs started to take shape, and she blinked the moisture from her eyes until she finally recognized the form standing in front of her.

"Aiza?"

"Oh, little sis, why couldn't you just leave well enough alone?"

"You're alive?"

"Yes, but you're going to get us both killed if you keep this up."

Sera wanted to reach out to her, but her hands were stuck at her sides, held in place by the rope tying her to the chair. She pulled against the rope, straining to break free, but the knots wouldn't budge.

She collapsed back against the chair, the throbbing in her head making it difficult to concentrate. She recognized her sister's face, her sister's voice, but there was something off about her. Something wrong that Sera couldn't quite grasp.

"Why am I tied up?"

"So you can't run away, silly."

"I'm not going to run away. I came here to find you." Which wasn't quite right, but it was true. "Aiza, please tell me what's going on."

"The perfect crime. Well, it was, until you started sniffing around. Why did you have to care so much? You didn't care for years and years, and now suddenly, I'm the most important person in your life?"

Sera blinked. "You were always important. I always cared. You're the one who stopped calling *me*. You're the one who started a new life and cut everybody out."

"So why didn't you take the hint? Why didn't you just go home, like everybody else?" Aiza asked harshly.

"I couldn't do that. Not when I thought you needed me."

"Well, I didn't need you. I don't need you. You're just getting in the way of everything."

"Okay, well, let me go home and I won't get in your way anymore. I'll just...I'll just act like everything's the same."

Aiza laughed—a cold sound—and shook her head. "What do you think? It's up to me? I couldn't let you go, even if I wanted to."

"Even if you wanted to? Aiza, look at me. Why can't you let me go?"

"Because we have to tie up all the loose ends. And you're a loose end."

"I'm not a loose end, I'm your sister! And I don't even *know* anything. All I know is that you're not in the ground and that's enough for me. Please, just let me go home."

Aiza's face softened, and for the first time, Sera didn't feel like she was staring into the eyes of a stranger. She held Aiza's gaze, hoping she would see what Sera meant every single word. It truly was enough for her to know that Aiza was not in that cold grave. She wouldn't press for more details or bring this meeting up to anybody.

"Sera," Aiza sighed. "I wish you had just gone home."

A crash outside the door stopped Sera's response. Another crash was followed by a howl of pain, quickly cut off with a wet, crunchy sound. Sera began struggling against the ropes again as Aiza went to the door, her hand going to the holster under her arm. Sera didn't know enough about guns to recognize the caliber, but the caliber didn't matter. She was armed and clearly prepared to use the weapon against whoever was on the other side of the door.

Who could it be but Seth?

The thought of Aiza putting a bullet in Seth's unsuspecting head drove Sera to her feet, despite the chair attached to her. She launched herself at her older sister, slamming her into the wall with enough force to put a dent in the plaster. At that moment, the door burst open, and both Sera and Aiza froze, their own skirmish forgotten.

Seth was still on two legs, but he was completely naked, covered in scratches, bites, bruises, and blood. Sera tried to say his name, but two wolves jumped on him in that moment, claws extended and teeth bared. Seth turned at the same moment they jumped and knocked one against the head with a closed fist. It hit the ground with a low whimper, but the other wolf was undeterred; it managed to seek its teeth into Seth's arm, ripping a chunk of flesh from his bicep.

"Seth!"

The sound of her voice may have broken Aiza from her trance. She sprung forward, the gun dropped and forgotten, her body morphing into that of a sleek, gray wolf, her mouth gaping open. Seth shifted just as she reached him, dropping low to the ground and allowing her to sail overhead. She couldn't stop her momentum before slamming into the wall, but that barely stunned her. She shook her head and jumped back to her feet, wheeling to face Seth again.

Sera had seen dog fights before, but she'd never seen anything like the brawl before her. The wolf that had attacked Seth first quickly fell away, a vicious bite to the ribs taking most of the fight out of him. But Aiza was brutal and she was fast. She moved like a gray blur, her lips curled all the way up to show her long, gleaming teeth. Seth was bigger, though, and he managed to stay out of her reach.

"Stop!" Sera shouted. "Stop, stop, stop. Please."

They may have heard her, but they were the past the point of understanding her. Blood had been drawn, and they were both wild with it, vicious and hungry for more. Still bound and tied, Sera began slamming the chair against the wall, doing her best to break it apart. She felt each blow all the way to her bones, but that didn't stop her from slamming her full weight into the chair again and again. Before long it cracked, and then it splintered, and the ropes holding her to the back began to loosen.

"Come on, come on," Sera muttered, slamming the chair into the wall again. Only feet away, her sister and her lover were tearing each other apart. Neither of them gave any sign of backing down, but both of them were dripping blood all over the floor. Their growls were loud enough to split her skull, and each chomp of their jaws sent a shiver down her spine.

Finally, the chair cracked and fell apart and she allowed the rope and wood to fall to her feet. Once she was free, she dove for the forgotten gun and fired it directly into the ceiling, hoping the unexpected explosion would shock the two wolves apart. The shot drew Aiza's attention long enough to give Seth the opening he needed, and he snapped forward as quickly as a snake, closing around her throat.

Sera fired again. "Stop! Let her go! Seth, let her go."

Sera had no idea how much Seth understood her when he was a wolf, or if he'd choose to listen to her even if he did understand. But she still had to try.

"Seth, please, she's my sister."

Seth relaxed his jaw and allowed Aiza's body to

drop to the ground at his feet. Sera bent at the knees, reaching forward to touch the blood-matted fur. She felt her sister's pulse and she could only hope that she stopped Seth in time. She didn't care what her sister got herself into, or even that Aiza might have intended to kill her.

"Sera!" Stephanie's voice seemed to come from a great distance. "Sera, come on. We have to keep moving."

"Seth..."

"I got him. Come on. The front door is just through there."

The gun felt hot and heavy against her palm, but she clutched it like a lifeline. She could see the front door, maybe thirty or forty feet ahead of her. It felt like thirty or forty miles. There were bodies on the floor. Some of them were clearly only injured, but a few were not moving at all, and Sera had a flash of understanding—Seth had done that. To get to her. He'd torn through all of them like they were made of nothing more than tissue.

Gotta get to the door, gotta get to the door, gotta get to the door.

She was so focused on the end goal, she didn't see the fist flying at her from the left. Stephanie's shout didn't give her enough warning to avoid the blow altogether, but she did duck enough that it caught her temple rather than smash her jaw. She dropped to one knee to avoid the next blow and slammed her elbow up, catching her assailant in the groin. The man groaned and dropped down, level with her. She drove the heel of her palm into the man's nose before he could get his bearings, and blood erupted from his nostrils.

Once Sera was on her feet, she saw the attacker was the infamous Dwight.

"Sera, let's go," Stephanie bit out.

"Wait." She leveled the gun at the man still lying at her feet. "I want an explanation."

"We don't have time for explanations," Stephanie protested.

But Sera wasn't listening. She didn't want to hear that. All she wanted to hear was *why*. Somebody was going to tell her the *why* of it before she stepped out the door. She grabbed the man by his collar and hauled him to his feet, giving him a good shake, the gun still pointed at his head.

"Dwight, I presume?"

"Bite me, bitch."

Sera reached without thinking, as though somebody else had taken over her body—a very, very angry somebody. She slammed the gun against

Dwight's jaw and pulled the barrel back, leveling at the spot between his eyes.

"Why attack me? Why fake Aiza's death?"

"I was trying to save your sister's life," Dwight said, his words slurring around broken teeth. "The Brotherhood had to believe she was dead. You got in the way."

"How did I get in the way?"

"Sera, come *on*," Stephanie said.

She heard the panic in Stephanie's voice and she understood they needed to hurry, but she couldn't pull herself away from the question. Her life had been flipped upside down and turned inside out. Everything had gone topsy-turvy since the news of Aiza's death, and now she stood there with a goose-egg developing on her head and a queasy feeling in her stomach and a gun in her hand, and dammit, she wanted to know *why*.

"You attract the wrong kind of attention," Dwight said.

Sera wanted to scream. That was no answer. But she didn't have the chance to force an actual answer. Stephanie shouted and then Seth made a high-pitched sound that might have been a cry of pain. Sera turned to look just in time to see Aiza throw herself at Seth's bleeding body. Dwight took advan-

tage of Sera's distraction and tackled her, driving her
to the ground. Sera grunted, the air driven out of her
lungs, and the world dimming around the edges. For
a moment, she thought she would black out, but
another howl from Seth pulled her back to reality.

She felt Dwight's weight shift and realized he was
becoming a wolf—a wolf that could rip her throat out.
Rip her stomach open. Rip her entire world apart.
The gun was still in her hand, and she knew what she
had to do. She never once thought of herself as a
killer. She'd never imagined herself in this moment or
even believed she would ever face the choice between
her life and another's. But this wasn't about her life.
This was about the life of her child. About the life of
her lover. This was about the life of her *pack*.

Once the decision was made, there was no
thinking left to do. Only action. She shot her elbow
backwards, trying to connect with Dwight's ribs. The
dull thud reverberated through her funny bone, but
she didn't let that slow her down. She did it again,
forcing the wolf back only a few inches, but it was
enough. She rolled onto her back, lifted the gun, and
fired at point blank range.

Sera had never fired a gun at a target. She'd
never fired at a living being. She didn't even know

how to aim, but at that distance, she could have fired with her eyes closed and hit the wolf in the face. He made a final yelping sound and then collapsed on her with his dead weight. Sera pushed the corpse away and jumped to her feet, the gun hotter than ever against her palm. She leveled the sites, but she couldn't get a clear shot at Aiza as she and Seth continued their earlier battle.

Sera was almost ready to shoot anyway when Seth finally struck the final blow, sending Aiza to the ground in a lifeless lump. The second her sister fell, Stephanie scooped Seth up in her arms, unmindful of his size and the blood and raced to the door, pausing for a moment to look back to Aiza's still form.

"Sera, come on. We have to go now."

Even now, she wanted to voice a protest, wanted to gather her sister up in her arms and carry her to the nearest hospital.

"Sera!" Seth called her name, and it was only the sound of his voice that pulled her from her fantasy of finally saving Aiza. She let the sound of his voice lure her away from the cabin and she stumbled down the walk after him, groping for him in the darkness. When he caught her, his hands were slick with blood, but his grip was strong and she knew he wouldn't let her go.

"There's a truck over there," Stephanie said. "Hurry."

Everything became a blur as Sera raced at Seth's side, hurrying towards their salvation. Seth pushed her into the front seat and Stephanie took the wheel, crowing triumphantly when she located the keys in the visor. Sera allowed herself one last look at the cabin as they sped away. She saw a shadow moving near the doorway, and she found herself hoping it was Aiza's. She stared until she couldn't see it anymore, until the cabin fell away from sight, swallowed by the moonless night.

10

Sera called her boss and told her that she would not be returning to work. Her boss begged her to reconsider, asked her if a raise would make her change her mind at all, and finally said with a sigh, "If you ever want to come back, you know where to find us." She called her landlord next and advised him she would not be renewing her monthly lease, and to keep the security deposit to cover any funds he was entitled to. She called her parents and didn't tell them anything important— she didn't mention Aiza, or the Wolf Brotherhood, or even Seth and the baby. She merely stated that she liked it in the northwest, and she would give them a call once she was settled.

After that, she spent a lot of time simply sitting quietly and thinking. Her guilt over her sister's demise was unquantifiable, even though she knew logically that it was none of her fault. Aiza had been an adult who made her own choices, and yet Sera couldn't help but think that her sister would still be alive if only she had gone home. If only she had listened to the sheriff when he warned her to let it go. If only she had listened to Seth when he warned her there were not people she wanted to be involved with.

The events in the cabin didn't make the news. No police came knocking on their door to demand an explanation for all the bodies, and though Seth upped security and warned his entire pack to be on the lookout for Brotherhood members, there was no sign of the biker gang.

"Won't they want revenge or something?" Sera asked.

"They likely want all of this to go away," Seth said. "We'll continue to be cautious, but I don't think we have anything to worry about."

But Sera disagreed. They had a lot to worry about. She was growing bigger by the day, and it was only the reality of her child that kept her grounded to earth, kept her eating, kept her sleeping, kept her sane.

"What do you think happened?" she asked Seth one night.

"I think Aiza stole money or drugs or guns from the Brotherhood. Or maybe Dwight did and she was his accomplice. Maybe she even took the fall for it and that's why they went through all the effort to fake her death."

"Did you kill her?"

"I don't know." Though the words were inconclusive, she knew they were honest.

"I hope she's still out there. I hope…"

"I know. Thank you, by the way."

"For what?"

"For putting your life at risk to save mine."

Sera snorted. "I nearly killed us all with that stunt. I should have stayed home and sat tight, like you said."

"Maybe. But you know what? Nobody's ever loved me enough to risk their life for me. You thought I was mad at you, but I wasn't."

"You weren't mad?" Sera asked.

"Of course not." He kissed the back of her neck and she felt herself relax against the heat of his mouth. "I mean, I wasn't happy that you would blindly stumble into a dangerous situation, but...I felt better when you were there. I feel good knowing you have my back."

"I'll always have your back," Sera said. "I love you."

"I love you, too." His hand went to her stomach. "And I love this little pup. When will you let me make it official?"

"Official? Are you asking me to marry you?"

"I am. I can't imagine my life without you, Sera." He paused for a moment, tears pricking the corners of his eyes. "Well, what do you think?"

"I think..." Sera took a deep breath. "I think I'd love to be your wife."

"So that's a yes?"

"It's a definite yes."

"Perfect. Just tell me what you want and it's yours," Seth said. "Your dream wedding."

"My dream wedding?" She could never have her dream wedding, because her dream wedding would include her entire family, but with this man, she'd have the wedding that she never dreamed was possible. And with him at her side, she would have the foundation for a new family. A close family full of love and support and kindness. A family like she never knew before. A *pack*. "Just as long as I have you, all my dreams will come true."

As she said the words, she realized how true they were. For as much as she lost, she'd gained the world.

PART III

THE WOLF PACK'S REVENGE

1

EVERYTHING WAS DARK AND EVERYTHING HURT. WHEN she pried her eyes open, there was light, and even the light hurt. Aiza couldn't locate the center of the pain, nor could she name it, describe it, or understand it. But it was her constant companion as she woke into a bloody, broken world.

She reached for something to hold on to. At first, she found only glass shards, and then finally, the shape of a familiar hand.

"Dwight?" She licked her lips and tried again, with a little more volume. "Dwight? Dwight, is that you?"

No response. Thinking she might have blacked out and missed a word or a twitch of his fingers, she tried again.

"Dwight? Dwight? What happened?"

Taking a deep breath, she forced herself to sit up. It was a slow process, but it still made her head spin. When the room finally righted itself, she saw that it *was* Dwight on the floor beside her.

Dwight was dead. She touched his neck, searching for his pulse. She couldn't remember exactly where to find the pulse, but he wasn't breathing and was covered in his own blood. Her gasp boiled over into a quick sob, but she stifled it, swallowing down the tears. She had no tears to shed for him. She cried for the memory of her sister's face—hurt, bruised, and scared, streaked with tears and blood.

Blood.

She'd made her baby sister bleed. No, she'd done worse than that.

She tried to kill her.

"Oh my God." Pain forgotten, she scrambled away from Dwight's corpse and tried to find her feet. Nothing was broken, but she bled from multiple wounds, and red and purple bruises bloomed across her ribs like roses. Her clothes were shredded and her feet had been sliced open on the wreckage of fatal violence.

"Oh my God."

She had to get out of there. With two bodies already behind her, she didn't dare get caught with a third—especially since she had no memory of what happened to him. Hell, she had no idea what happened to *herself*, or what she might have done. If she could attack Sera, she was clearly capable of anything.

There was another sign of a struggle in her bedroom. The sight of the broken chair, the blood on the floor, the dent in the wall—it was all too much. She couldn't even step past the door. She considered forgoing clothes and shifting into her wolf form, but the thought sent a shudder through her stomach.

A now musty load of clothes forgotten in the washer was her only salvation—a damp pair of jeans and one of Dwight's flannel shirts hid most of her hastily bandaged wounds. No amount of make-up could cover the black eye or swollen lip, but she still tried.

Dwight's truck was parked haphazardly in the driveway, keys still in the ignition. Sera's scent had been strong in the cabin, and she still caught traces in the yard, but after a certain point, it was gone. Clearly, they'd left in another vehicle, and in the distance, she saw lights that may have been them, but she had no hope of catching up.

Even if she did catch up, what would she say? How could she possibly explain? She knew Dwight's influence had something to do with it, but she couldn't quite remember what he said—and she certainly didn't know *why*. She couldn't explain herself. She couldn't explain anything. She just wanted to go home, shower, sleep and face this nightmare by the light of day.

The old truck was a bitch to drive and she was weak from exhaustion. Her adrenaline was enough to get her on the road, but not enough to sustain her, and more than once, the wheel jerked from her hands. She tried to correct it, but in her panic, she over-corrected and felt the tires skid from the smooth pavement to the rough gravel.

Another rough yank to the wheel almost had her back on the road, but a post stood between her and the pavement. The truck slammed to a hard stop, yanking her forward.

The next thing she heard was a tap on the window. Blinking up against the light, she tried to make out the face on the other side of the glass, but she couldn't see anything behind the glare.

"Ma'am? Ma'am? Are you okay?"

"I...I don't know. I think so."

He pulled the truck door open and she fell out rather than stepped out. Directly into his arms. Her fingers closed around his leather jacket, and gradually, her breathing returned to normal. But her heart still thudded in her ears, and her tears rolled unchecked down her cheeks. Normally, she would not allow herself to sob pathetically in a strange man's arms, but being completely overwhelmed physically, mentally, and emotionally, she didn't have the wherewithal to break free and stand on her own two feet.

Gradually, the tears slowed, then stopped, and finally she could breathe normally again. Only then did he gently hold her away from him.

"I'm sorry about that," she said, trying to wipe her nose. "I'm sorry. I'm fine. You can...I'll just call..."

He produced a handkerchief from his pocket and pressed it into her palm. She offered a watery smile of gratitude before wiping her eyes and nose.

"What's your name?" The man asked.

"Aiza Simpson."

"Simpson?"

Aiza nodded.

He gently touched the side of her cheek. "You're hurt. I can take you to the hospital..."

"No," she said quickly. "No hospitals. I'm fine. I promise."

"This shiner didn't happen just now, did it? Did somebody attack you?" His face was creased with concern, his voice full of worry, and his eyes so sincere that she wanted nothing more than to trust him. But she was only in this situation because she had trusted the wrong man in the first place, and her heart was already starting to harden against the stranger's charms.

"I...my boyfriend....attacked me. He just went crazy and I thought he was going to kill me." She buried her face against the man's chest, cooling her flushed cheeks on his rain-dampened jacket. "So I...he's...I fought back and he fell and I...I took his truck..." The lie came easily, fueled as it was by necessity. "Please, he might be coming after me. I need to get out of here. I need—"

"Ms. Simpson, you need to get to a hospital. I'll drive you to the emergency room. Come on." He guided her to the passenger door of his car and assisted her inside.

"No! I mean...I'm scared that's where he'll look for me. If you could just give me a ride to a hotel or something—"

"I can take you somewhere safe. Not fancy, but safe."

Aiza looked behind her shoulder to the old truck. The pole dented the bumper, but she was sure she could still drive it. The question was, did she even *want* to drive it? She'd lost control of it once; who could say she wouldn't lose control again? And if she did, she might do a lot worse than hitting a random pole at low speed. She might hit a tree the next time. Or a person. And she sure didn't need another life on her conscience.

He took her silence as accession and led her by the arm to his car. The motor was still running and the interior was warm and comfortable. She sighed and leaned back in the seat, letting the warm air dry her tear-stained cheeks and rain-soaked hair.

"I'm sorry, I didn't catch your name," Aiza said once he slid behind the wheel.

"Noah Longtail."

"Nice to meet you, Noah." She looked over her shoulder. "What about the truck?"

"I can call for a tow truck."

"I..." She hated that ugly thing. What did she need it for? She doubted anybody would bother to steal it—and if they did, good riddance. If not, it could rot there just like Dwight. "I'll have a friend take care of it in the morning."

"Are you sure you don't want to go to the hospital? We're not far."

"I'm sure. I promise if I start to feel light-headed or anything I'll tell you and you can take me right to the emergency room."

He nodded. "Fair enough." He gestured at the radio. "You can put on something, if you'd like."

She accepted the kind gesture and searched through the stations for something, but none of the music was soothing and all the commercials were loud and jarring. She flicked the dial off and stared out the window. She was sure he would have more questions for her once they stopped. Questions she wouldn't want to answer. Questions she didn't even know *how* to answer.

Would he be so nice to her when they discovered Dwight's dead body? Or Butch's? Or Franklin's? She knew she didn't kill Dwight, but the circumstances didn't look good. They didn't look good at all.

Oh, I'm fucked.

Fear stabbed through her, sharp enough to make her cry out. She tried to swallow down her sob before he heard—but he definitely heard it.

"Ma'am? I want you to know, you're safe now."

Sure, sure thing. Absolutely. I'm safe now. A hollow lie, no matter who said it. She couldn't nod, she couldn't agree with him...she couldn't even acknowledge she heard him.

Safe. What did that word even mean? After everything she'd been through, she didn't think she'd feel safe ever again.

"I think he's dead," she said numbly. "I...I didn't kill him, though."

"Who killed him?"

"I don't know. I didn't catch his name. At least...I don't think I did."

"Was there an intruder?"

"No...well, yes, but...no." Aiza held her head, her temples throbbing. She had a sudden spin of vertigo, and for a moment, she thought she might throw up. "God, my head is killing me."

"Do you need me to pull over?"

She tried to shake her head, but the smallest motion sent another shard of pain through her temple. "I don't know."

"If you need to puke, let me know," he said with a small smile. "Look, maybe we should go to the police."

Her immediate reaction was to say *no*, but she bit

that back. "In the morning. Please. I just need to rest."

Noah nodded and she rested her head against the cool window. Her stomach was still roiling, her head hurt and her sides ached. He didn't speak again and she was grateful for the silence.

2

NEARLY THIRTY MINUTES AFTER HE PICKED HER UP, Noah came to a stop in front of what appeared to be a truly massive house.

"Is this yours?"

"No, I rent a room here. Sit tight, I'll help you out."

He came around to the passenger side and wrapped one arm around her shoulder, gently lifting her from the seat. She leaned heavily on him, and he practically carried her around the corner to the side entrance. The door opened to a narrow hallway, and he guided her to the final door, keeping his hold on her as he unlocked the door.

The room was small but meticulously kept. The only furniture included a bed—carefully made—an old recliner, and a television. He brought her to the bed and left her seated on the mattress.

"Were you in the military?"

"Marine. How did you know?"

"Just a hunch."

"We should get you out of those clothes."

"*What*?"

Noah grimaced. "I'm sorry, that came out wrong. Your clothes are wet. I have a nice dry robe. Why don't you go change and I'll make you something to drink."

"Do you have whiskey?"

"Yup."

"Perfect." Aiza pushed herself to her feet, refusing his offer of help. "I'll take a big glass of whiskey. Point me in the right direction."

He pointed her in the direction of a washroom the size of a very small closet. The sink, toilet, and shower were the sort you might find in a small RV. She couldn't imagine a man the size of Noah trying to wedge himself into the tiny shower every morning. The robe he offered her was several sizes too large, but she was happy to wrap herself in its soft folds, cinching the belt in a tight knot to keep it secure.

A brief glance in the mirror was all she needed to

see that the accident in the truck added another bruise to her face. She ran her fingers through her tangled hair and splashed her face with water, but she still looked like an utter mess. Somehow, as bad as she looked, she felt even worse.

"I hope you have that whiskey ready for me," she said as she emerged from the bathroom.

"Of course," he said, placing a hand on her shoulder to guide her to the La-Z-Boy. Beside it was a tray holding a glass of whiskey, a mug with a tea bag, and a bowl of soup. "I didn't know if you were hungry, but I figured it couldn't hurt."

"Thank you. You didn't have to go to all this trouble."

"It's not any trouble. I'm just being a good host."

"No." Aiza shook her head. "You're being an angel." Tears welled up in her eyes and she tried to blink them away, but her emotions couldn't be stifled. "You're being so nice and I don't deserve it."

He crouched beside the chair, directly in her field of vision. She had no choice but to look directly in his eyes—they were green, she noticed for the first time. "Don't talk like that. I don't know what you've been through or what that boyfriend of yours has done to you, but you *do* deserve basic kindness and a hell of a lot more than that."

"You don't understand. I've done...I've done some really bad things."

Noah covered her hand with his much larger one. The back of his hand was covered in a deep tan and several much lighter scars. His fingers were warm, his skin smooth, and though she felt undeniable strength in his hand, his hold was unbelievably gentle. Her nostrils flared and she caught a scent that was both familiar and strange. She tensed and he immediately moved his hand away.

"Wait." She caught his hand and briefly squeezed his fingers. "Are you—?"

"What?"

"Are you a *werewolf*?"

He tilted his head, studying her for a moment. "I am. I reckon you're one, too."

She nodded.

"You haven't been one for long, though?" Noah guessed.

"No. Just this year."

"Was your boyfriend a wolf?"

Aiza nodded.

"Did he make you?"

Aiza nodded again. Noah mimicked the motion, like he got the answer he expected. "Will you do me a favor?"

"What?"

"Will you eat your soup?"

"I will," she said, but she reached for the whiskey. She gulped down half the glass before picking up the bowl. The broth had cooled enough to eat, and once she started, she realized how hungry she was. She couldn't remember the last time she ate anything, and her stomach growled loud enough to make Noah smile.

"Just let me know if you want another bowl. There's plenty more where that came from."

"Did you make this?" Aiza asked.

"No, a friend of mine did. She brought me a whole gallon."

"What do you need with so much soup?"

"She's worried I'll starve otherwise." He shrugged. "There's a McDonald's down the block, but I guess that's not good enough."

"This is *definitely* better than McDonald's," she murmured before taking another bite. She nearly inhaled the soup and gulped down the rest of the whiskey before speaking again.

"Thank you. I feel much better now."

He took the bowl and glass from her and she

pushed herself to her feet, excusing herself to the bathroom. She was still struggling to tie up the oversized robe when she emerged, and by his sudden intake of breath, she knew he caught sight of the abrasions on her ribs. Some of them were bleeding again, and she'd tried to clean them up as much as possible, but she needed bandages.

"Good God, Aiza. Let me look at those."

"No, it's okay," she said, holding the robe closed with a tight fist. "I'm okay."

"Aiza, you're bleeding and you need to be bandaged. I have a first aid kit. Please let me help you."

She swallowed, realizing it was rather silly to let her wounds seep blood all night, and nodded. She sat on the bed and shrugged her right arm out of the robe, allowing the terry to fall open and expose the worst of the claw marks.

"That looks like a pretty bad fight," he said.

"It wasn't a good one."

"This is going to sting a little."

It stung a lot, actually, but Aiza didn't visibly react. She overlooked the sting to focus on the gentle pressure of Noah's fingers as he efficiently cleaned the claw wounds. The sudden coolness of the antibiotic balm brought a gasp to her lips and he gave her a sharp look.

"Are you okay?"

"Yeah, I'm good." She offered a reassuring smile. "I'm actually feeling better already."

He searched her face for a moment and then returned to his task. When he finished with the right side, she moved so he could focus on her back.

"He bit you."

"I...I didn't realize."

"This might need stitches, Aiza. You should really go to the ER."

"I'll go to the clinic tomorrow," she promised. "I need sleep more than anything. This will heal itself in no time."

He didn't offer another argument, and soon he had her completely bandaged, her ribs wrapped in tape. "I'll reheat your tea." He pulled a T-shirt from the top drawer of his dresser. "Get comfortable. I'll be right back."

When he returned, she was curled up on his surprisingly comfortable mattress, nestled under the soft blanket. "Where are you going to sleep?"

"I'm not." He offered her the mug. "I was on my way to a meeting when I saw you go off the road and they're still waiting for me."

"So, you're leaving?"

"For a few hours. But I'll lock the door behind me, and I promise you, no one will bother you here."

Aiza nodded, too tired to argue. Her head was already on the pillow and her eyes were already falling closed. The last thing she was aware of was the lock of the door clicking shut.

3

By the time Aiza woke, her bruises were beginning to fade and the worst of the open wounds were starting to close, no stitches necessary. The room seemed homier in the warm afternoon sunlight. She stayed in the comfortable bed for a long time after she woke up, a part of her wishing she could just remain there forever. She felt safe and comfortable, warm and secure.

Hunger and a full bladder eventually drove her from the warm bed. Noah was nowhere to be seen, but she found more soup and cold beer in the fridge, and she helped herself to both. There was still pain in her ribs and neck, but she could move freely and she knew it wouldn't be too much longer until she felt like herself again.

But what would happen after that?

She wanted to step back into her life, but could that even be possible now that her life was legally over? Aiza wasn't sure about the legal implications of faking her own death, but she had the feeling it would just be one more thing for the district attorney to bring up in court.

With no phone, no money, and no idea where she even was, Aiza felt a little like a prisoner. She paced around the small apartment and even ventured into the narrow hallway, but the sudden scent of a dozen wolves drove her back, the door closing quickly behind her. She had no way of knowing if the other wolves were friend or foe, and she wasn't in a hurry to find out. With no other options, Aiza crawled back into bed and almost immediately returned to sleep.

When she woke up again, she wasn't alone.

"How are you feeling?" Noah asked.

"Better." She gently ran her fingers over her ribs. "Much better."

"Good. I'm glad to hear it. Are you hungry?"

"Yeah. I helped myself to some soup earlier."

He smiled. "That's fine, that's what it's there for. I ordered some Chinese and it should be here soon. Let me have a look at those bandages."

She patiently allowed his inspection, performing one of her own while he was distracted with his task. His face was even more handsome than she remembered, his brow creased with concentration, his full mouth set in a thin line. In the light, she could see his hair was closer to blonde than brown, and pale whiskers sprouted across his chin and cheeks. He wore a dark T-shirt pulled tightly over his broad shoulders and solid chest, and the memory of what that chest felt like made her shiver.

"Are you okay?" he asked.

"Oh, yeah, just a little chilly."

He helped her replace her clothes and stood up with a small nod. "You're going to be fine. Is there anybody you'd like to call? Or maybe I can give you a ride somewhere?"

"I'd appreciate a ride home." She frowned. "Where are we?"

"Yakima."

"Oh. Do you mind taking me all the way back to Portland?"

He shook his head. "I don't mind at all."

"Thanks. I appreciate that and, well, everything. More than you can know."

A knock on the door pulled his attention from her, and as soon as she caught a whiff of the Chinese food, her stomach cramped with hunger. She felt like she hadn't taken a bite in weeks and began to devour an order of boneless spare ribs. Noah didn't seem to mind, though he did eat his skewer of teriyaki beef a considerably slower pace. A few times, she caught him watching her with a strange smile on his face, as though she were a particularly amusing sort of puzzle.

"Before we head to Portland, I was hoping you'd come to my office," he said as he reached for a second skewer.

Aiza paused between swallows. "Your office? Why would I want to go to your office?"

"To make a statement."

"A statement?" Her eyes widened. "You're a cop."

"Well, no, I'm not a cop. But I am a federal officer."

Aiza's involuntary gasp drew a piece of pork down her throat and quickly turned into a ragged cough. He jumped to his feet to her assist her, slapping her between the shoulders to dislodge the food.

"What...you're a...a federal officer?"

"I work for H.O.W.L. Have you heard of it?"

"Homeland Department of Wolfs and Lycanthropes," Aiza stated numbly.

"Yes. We've been investigating the Wolf Brotherhood and your old friend Dwight for a very long time."

"So...you didn't just happen to find me, did you?"

Noah shook his head.

"You were following me."

"We've been staking out his cabin for some time," Noah said.

"So...you knew about the attack, too?"

"Yes. I know a great many things, Aiza, and you don't have to be afraid of me. I want to help you."

"How can you help me?" Aiza demanded. "I'm...I'm guilty, too."

"Guilty of what? Being Dwight's accomplice?"

"Yes, for starters."

"Aiza, you and I both know that Dwight forced you to do things."

"Forced? He never...he never forced me. I...I made my own decisions."

"Including the decision to attack your sister?" Noah asked softly.

"How did you know about that?"

"I told you, I know a great many things. He told you to attack her, didn't he?"

Aiza nodded slowly.

"He planted that suggestion as your maker. God knows what else he planted in your head. Now that he's dead, his control over you will fade. Make a statement. Explain what happened. Then instead of being a suspect, you'll be a witness."

"Against who? Dwight is dead."

"Against the Brotherhood."

"Oh no. Oh no, no, no. I'm tired of them tangling in my business and I don't want to have anything to do with them. If I testify against them, they'll catch wind that I'm actually still alive and they'll come after me."

"We'll keep you safe," Noah promised. "*I'll* keep you safe."

Aiza shook her head. "Excuse me if I'm not impressed with the promise. I mean, they attacked me in my own home. How will you stop them?"

"Well, for starters, I'll make sure they can't find you."

"So...if I help you, I can't go home."

"Not right away," Noah conceded. "But when it's all over, you can go back to your home. Your bar. Your life."

"My bar," she murmured. "You already know everything, don't you? What will happen to me if I don't cooperate? Will I be placed under arrest?"

"Not by me, certainly. But the local authorities

might have different ideas. Especially if they're on the take."

"So, if I tell you everything I know about Dwight and the Brotherhood and...everything, I won't be sent to jail?"

"No, you will be given full immunity and protection." Noah leaned forward, his eyes serious, and she had no choice but to meet his gaze. She felt like he was looking right through her, and it was impossible not to squirm under the weight of his stare—until she realized that he wasn't trying to pick her apart; he was giving her the chance to read his face, and even his soul, before she made her decision.

"Okay." Aiza took a deep breath. "I'll do it."

His face broke into a wide smile. It was the nicest smile she had ever seen, and under any other circumstances, it would have been impossible not to return the gesture. "You made the right choice. I promise you."

"Are we going to do this now?"

"If you're ready. Or you can rest here for another night and we'll head over first thing in the morning."

Aiza opted for the morning, thinking that would give her time to gather her thoughts and prepare herself, but she passed the whole night in nervous agony. Noah disappeared again just after ten—no doubt on official business—giving her plenty of space and time to sleep, but instead she tossed and turned on the narrow bed, seeing Dwight's face every time she closed her eyes. She tried to reason with herself; she tried to accept that she would be truly free of him, but an unidentifiable dread settled in her stomach and make itself at home there.

Noah returned the next morning just after dawn with coffee and bagels. Aiza was already awake and dressed when he opened the door, and he didn't comment on the bags under her eyes or the carefully made bed. She ate in grateful silence, her appetite still making itself known despite the nerves twisting her stomach into knots.

Once she was done, she signaled her readiness and he led her to the car. He walked with long, deliberate strides, his posture perfect, his carriage one of supreme confidence. The sun caught the blonde highlights in his hair and the golden hue of his skin, and she had the feeling he spent far more time outside than he did sitting behind a desk. It was easy to imagine him fishing beside a mountain stream or rock climbing or sailing.

"Who else will be there?" Aiza asked, wondering if he could hear the tremor in her voice.

"My partner, Dana."

"Should I have a lawyer?"

"You're not being charged with anything, but you're welcome to have an attorney present."

"I have one...I mean, I know one. He's not a criminal attorney, though. He worked with me when I purchased the bar."

"I can help you find one."

"But I'm not being charged, you said."

"Not a public defender. There are plenty of wolves who provide their services *pro bono*. I know a few; I can call them when we get there." He offered her a reassuring smile. "I want you to be comfortable, Aiza. You're going to be a very big help to us."

"Thank you." It *did* seem like a good idea to at least consult with a lawyer before she spilled her guts and incriminated herself. Why would they offer her full immunity when Dwight was already dead? She didn't know anything else about the rest of the Brotherhood—the only members she ever met, she killed. It was in self-defense, true, but what proof did she have of that?

Only the truth. The whole truth. And nothing but the truth.

With bathroom breaks, water breaks, and crying breaks, it took a little over four hours to get through the entire story. Noah remained standing for most of it, his face set in a pensive mask as his partner, Dana O'Driscoll, asked questions to guide Aiza's long narrative.

She started at the beginning, the night she met Dwight, and continued through the details of her accident, her damaged memory, and her decision to be made into a werewolf. That was the easy part.

After she started talking about the night Butch came to her bar and demanded money, and then attacked her, she couldn't look at Noah any longer. She couldn't meet Dana's eyes, either. She just stared at her hands and recited as much as she could remember. By the time she detailed the attack that killed Franklin, she felt winded and sick to her stomach with shame and fear. It seemed to her that she gave them no choice. They would have to arrest her when she confessed that Dwight convinced her not to call the police, to just let him hide the bodies, like it was no big deal.

She half-expected her new attorney to stop her story, but he allowed her to continue speaking without interruption. He'd introduced himself as Sam Longtail, and Aiza's eyes had darted to Noah's face, searching for a family resemblance. Maybe it was only a coincidence, but Yakima wasn't *that* big and the name wasn't that common. But if they were related, her guess would be distant cousins.

Finally, she ran out of things to say and Dana ran out of questions to ask her. She stood and offered her hand with a small smile that reached her eyes. "I wish we'd met under different circumstances, Ms. Simpson, but I'm very grateful you chose to come in and speak with us today."

"Oh, um, you're welcome. I hope I can actually help with your investigation. I never meant...I'm not a murderer."

Dana's warm grip tightened and her smile turned reassuring. "It will help and we know you're not a murderer. Now if you'll excuse me for just a moment, I need to talk to my partner."

They stepped into the hall and Aiza turned to Sam, looking for any sign of what to expect next.

"It sounds like you've had a hell of a year," he said.

"It's been rough. I just hope the next year isn't spent in jail."

"Don't worry about it," Sam said confidently. "You did the world a favor when you removed those mutts from it. And those two have bigger fish to try. Noah said he's going to keep you safe, and he will."

As if summoned by his words, Noah reappeared. "Are you ready to move?"

"Where are we going?"

"A safe house we've got ready for you." He looked to Sam. "I'll be in touch."

She followed Noah out of the room, her heart still hammering in her ears. She didn't feel better until they were in the car and the building was several miles behind them. "Where's the house?"

"It's best if you don't know."

"What do you think I'm going to do? Call the Brotherhood and tell them where to find me?"

"No, but a secret safe house is a secret safe house. Until everybody knows the secret."

"Why not just blindfold me then?"

"I will if I think it's necessary," he said lightly.

She smiled despite herself and let it drop. It didn't really matter to her where the safe house was or why he wanted to keep the location a secret, as long as she was safe and had a place to heal and figure out her life.

He took her north, further from Portland and the Brotherhood's territory. She never spent much time in Washington, so she could gauge the direction but not the location. He slowed down to thirty miles per hour as they entered a tiny town and began pointing out different places of interest—the general store, the bank, the post office, and the local watering hole. Finally, he pulled to a stop in front of a bungalow at the outskirts of town.

"Home sweet home."

It looked nice enough on the outside. The house had been recently painted white with green trim, the yard was well cared for and bursting with flowers, and a tall oak tree cast a long shadow over the front porch. He opened the car door for her and moved to the trunk where he pulled out several bags of groceries, loading his arms before moving to the front door.

"The key is in my pocket," he said, nodding towards his right leg.

"Oh...um." She delicately reached past the tight lip of his pocket, sliding her fingers down his hard thigh in search of the key. She snatched it and quickly pulled her hand back, her cheeks suddenly suffused with heat. Ducking her head so he wouldn't notice her strangely flustered reaction, she unlocked the house and pushed the door open. He stepped in first, turning off the security system and flipping on the lights before gesturing for her to follow.

"I'll teach you how to use all of this. But I promise, you'll never wake up with a stranger in your room again."

"The alarm is that good, huh?"

"Nobody will even get this far. There are sensors all along the perimeter of the property. They are rigged to set off silent alarms that'll bring down a team of armed men like the wrath of an angry god."

Her eyes darted out the open door. "There's a team watching the house?"

"Yes."

"Where are they?"

Noah smiled and gently closed the door. "There will also be a two-man detail assigned to you at all times."

"I'm going to be followed twenty-four hours a day?"

"For your own safety."

"But only for, like, a couple of months, right?" His eyes darted away and she felt her heart sink. "You don't think this is only going to be for a few months, do you?"

"There's no way of knowing," Noah said. "If it were up to me, I'd have every mongrel and cur locked up by tonight. But it's not up to me. Come on, let me show you around."

There wasn't much to show. It was a single level

home with one bedroom, one bath, and a kitchen split from the living room by a wet bar. The carpet was a neutral beige, the walls all a bland white, and the furniture was far from plush.

"I know it's not much, but it's got a satellite dish and Wi-Fi."

"Wonderful."

"The fridge is fully stocked," he said, opening the door to show a fridge that was, indeed, full of food. None of it looked like anything she wanted to deal with, though. What was she going to do with a whole chicken, raw spinach, and a giant pork roast? She usually survived on cereal, burgers, and whiskey.

"The store is only a mile down the road," he said, as if sensing her thoughts. "And you'll be provided with an expense card. You can decorate the place. Hang a few things up on the walls. Make it more like a home."

"Yeah, I'll think about it." She didn't have any desire to make the place homier. She *had* a home. "What about you? Will you be staying here with me?

"I'll be checking in on you often. And I have a phone for you with my number programmed in. If you need anything, call me anytime."

"So, you're just going to leave me alone up here? Can I let anybody know I'm here?"

Noah shook his head. "Everybody thinks you're dead, Aiza, and until we wrap up our investigation, it's safer for you if they keep thinking it."

She saw there was no point in arguing so she inclined her head. "I guess that'll give me plenty of time to...reflect on what I've done."

"Hey." He reached out, resting his hand lightly on her shoulder. She automatically leaned into the friendly touch, drawn to both the warmth of his skin and the strength she could sense in his long fingers. "I know it seems bad now."

"Not as bad as jail," Aiza said. "So it could be worse."

"It could be worse," Noah agreed. "But I promise, I'll make it better."

"Why do you keep saying things like that?"

"Like what?"

"Promising to help me, keep me safe, and make things better. Are you just, like, the world's nicest guy or something?" He was still holding her shoulder, and for the first time, she realized how close they were standing. She wanted to move in even closer; wanted him to wrap both of his arms around her and hold her because she had the feeling he actually *was* the world's nicest guy.

"No, I'm just a decent man who believes in helping those who need help."

"In my experience, there's not many decent men around. Not when you need them."

"Then I'm grateful our paths crossed."

"Grateful?"

"So I can be the one who gives you a new experience." He squeezed her shoulder gently and then stepped back. "I'm sorry I have to go, but I'll be back in the morning."

He did return the next morning, bringing bagels, juice, and a half dozen thick books. "These are my favorites" he told her. "They got me through some rough times. Maybe they can help you, too."

Every time he returned after that, he brought her something new to help her pass the time. She welcomed the books, the DVDs and the distractions, but she found—more than anything—it was his company, his smile, and his warmth that made each day better and better.

4

On the morning of their wedding day, Seth woke Sera with soft, sweet kisses against her neck. She smiled sleepily and tilted her head back, allowing him to nuzzle his lips over her pulse and under her ear. His hand rested on her hip, pulling her back against his body, his long leg draped over hers. He slid his palm up her ribs, coming to rest on her larger-than-normal breast. He sighed as he cupped its weight, her nipple hard against the palm of his hand.

She shifted, her ass coming to rest more firmly against his growing erection. He couldn't help but move his own hips, grinding against her, seeking more heat, more pressure. Despite his growing hunger, his lips were still slow, gliding over her neck and shoulder as he took deep breaths, savoring her scent, both familiar and new.

This was how they woke most mornings, wrapped in each other's arms, mouths seeking contact, bodies still supple with sleep. It was strange to see the same person every day, to go to sleep content because that person was there, and to wake smiling and aching for more contact.

He'd never met anybody he craved like he craved Sera. He even dreamed about her.

He wanted Sera near him at all times—a sharp deviation from how he used to run his life, but one his pack members had become accustomed to. Stephanie had helped considerably with that, as she had realized right away that Sera was different—not only from his previous one-night stands and flings, but also from the pack. He loved his pack; he cared for every one of his wolves and devoted his life to them, but that was instinctual due to the wolf inside of him. It was the *man* who found Sera; who yearned for her and loved her.

"Oh," she gasped, and he knew that it wasn't a sound of pleasure. "He's got a lot of energy this morning."

Seth moved his hand to her stomach. He didn't

have to wait long to feel the powerful kick of his son. "He's really got a strong pair of legs on him."

"Yes, he does."

"Maybe he'll be a soccer player like his old man."

She looked over her shoulder. "You played soccer?"

"In high school."

"Were you any good?" Sera asked with a smile.

"I was the team captain."

She laughed. "Of course you were."

"Why is that funny?"

"Did you ever participate in anything without being the captain, or president, or Alpha?"

Seth considered the question for a moment before answering with an honest, "No."

"Yeah, that's what I thought. What time is it?"

He pulled her closer. "Why?"

"Because I have to get up."

"No you don't."

"Yes I do." She covered his fingers with hers but didn't try to move his hand away. "I have one more dress fitting this morning, and then there are a million things to do before the ceremony tonight."

He lifted his head, frowning. "A million things to do?"

"To supervise," she quickly amended. "You know

Stephanie and everybody else has been such a big help with getting everything taken care of."

"I still think we should have waited," Seth said. Not because he had any desire to delay being married, but because the doctor had already warned Sera she needed to take it easy, stay off her feet, and rest as much as possible. She set the date, insisting it needed to be before the baby was born, despite the inherent stress of planning a wedding. She'd also rejected his suggestion that they have a quick, private ceremony at the courthouse, stating that since she was only going to do this once, she was going to do it right. What choice did he have but to agree?

"I don't think I can even stand to wait another day to be your wife," she said, kissing the corner of his mouth. "Just think. At this time tomorrow, I'll be Mrs. Seth Longtail."

"Just think?" Seth grinned. "I can't stop thinking about it." His grin turned lascivious and he attacked her neck with playful bites. "Or the honeymoon."

She laughed. "Stop! Stop!"

"Really?"

"No. But, yes." She pressed a kiss to his mouth. "Stephanie is going to be here in less than thirty minutes."

"You know, that's plenty of time," Seth said.

"Not if I want to shower, do my morning yoga, and eat a healthy breakfast," Sera reminded him.

He relented, relaxing his arms and allowing her to scoot to the edge of the bed and swing her feet over the side. He had his own busy day ahead of him, with plenty of things to do before the bonding ceremony that night, but he still lingered in bed, watching silently as she performed her morning regimen. He couldn't explain why—she had asked several times—but he loved to simply watch her complete the most mundane tasks. He noted every moment of her brushing her teeth, taming her hair into a ponytail, bending her way through fifteen minutes of yoga, and stripping to take a quick shower.

Once she was under the spray, he made his way to the kitchen. He was in the habit of cooking for her at least once a day, though he preferred to see to all of her meals. Today he made an egg and bacon frittata, served with a fruit smoothie and a Greek yogurt with a touch of raw honey. By the time she emerged, the freshly plated food was waiting for her on the table.

"Thank you. This looks so good." She tilted her chin up for a quick kiss, and he couldn't help but deepen the kiss, prolonging the contact for as long as he could.

"Eat up. You'll need the protein."

"Yes sir."

He checked the clock and swore softly. He was already running behind, which was his own damned fault. But he wouldn't have changed a thing—well, that's not true. He would have stayed in bed even longer if she'd been willing.

"I have to go to my office this morning to see to a few more things before we go out of town. But I'll be back here by one. Two at the latest," Seth said.

"Okay."

"Call me if you need anything at all. I'll pick it up on the way home."

"Will do."

"Be sure to drink plenty of water, take breaks, don't do anything too strenuous."

"Honey?"

"Yes."

Sera smiled. "Please relax. I'm fine. The baby is fine. Everything is fine, and tonight, everything is going to be perfect. Okay?"

Seth bent to kiss her smile. "Okay. I love you."

"Knock knock," Stephanie said as she stepped

through the back door. "I hope somebody is ready for her fitting."

"I am. Is Peggy here?"

Peggy was the seamstress making the dress. Sera had never had an article of clothing to order before, and she'd been thrilled to collaborate on designing a beautiful dress appropriate for the bonding ceremony. Sera had balked a little at the additional expense of having a hand-sewn dress, but Peggy was a member of the pack, and Jackie had insisted. Jackie was the wedding planner that Seth had insisted on.

"She is. She's on the phone." Stephanie wrapped her arm around Seth in a friendly hug. "I see you are literally hovering over her now."

"Just to say goodbye." He returned the hug and then grabbed his keys and wallet from the counter. "Make sure she drinks enough water and stays off her feet."

"And doesn't stress out, or pick anything up, or move. I know the drill."

Seth gave his co-Alpha and pack sister an affectionate smile before pulling himself away and hurrying out the door. They weren't siblings, but they were born within a week of each other, raised together from birth, and best friends from the beginning. He knew most of his pack expected the two of them to marry one day. It made sense when he looked at it from their point of view—they were already co-Alphas and nearly inseparable—but for the two of them, it had never been an option. She was his sister in all ways but blood. There was nobody else on Earth that he would trust with his mate and his unborn child.

His phone rang, pulling him from his thoughts. "Hey, Noah. What's the word?"

"Nothing good, I'm afraid."

"What happened?"

"I'd rather not tell you over the phone."

Seth swore under his breath.

"When can I expect you?" Noah asked.

"I'm on my way right now."

5

SERA'S SMILE FADED FROM HER FACE AS SOON AS SETH left and that did not escape Stephanie's sharp eye.

"What's wrong?" Stephanie asked without preamble.

"Nothing. Everything is great."

"You certainly don't look like everything is great, and you sure don't look like somebody who's about to get married." Stephanie took the seat opposite of her. "So tell me the truth. What's on your mind?"

Sera sighed. She knew it wouldn't do any good to lie to her friend. Stephanie had an unerring ability to detect bullshit and call people on it.

"Aiza. She's alive out there, somewhere. Maybe." She swallowed hard. Her emotions were always closer to the surface these days, and tears were already stinging the corners of her eyes.

"I can't stop thinking about her," Sera continued. "We just left her there. Alone. Anything could have happened to her. How could I just leave her?"

"Sera, we—"

"We left her. We should have brought her with us. We should have helped her or gone back for her. And here I am getting married and planning the rest of my life like I didn't betray her."

"You *didn't* betray her," Stephanie said. "She tried to kill you. She tried to kill all of us. After she lied to you about being dead." She shook her head. "I know you love her. She's your sister. But you're not to blame for this."

"But that's just it. Something was *clearly* wrong with her. If she can't count on me to defend her and protect her and figure out what's wrong, then who can she count on?"

"Sera, from what you've told me, she hasn't counted on you in a very long time." Stephanie leaned forward, wrapping her arm around Sera's shoulders and pulling her into a hug. "She's an adult who made her own choices. You don't have to bear the burden of those choices."

Sera returned the hug with a grateful sigh,

though she still felt like her heart was breaking. The past five months had been the best and worst of her life. She'd never been happier. She didn't even know it was possible to be so happy. Waking up in Seth's arms every day, carrying his child and building a new life beyond her sweetest fantasies were blessings she couldn't even account for. But every happy moment was tainted, tinged by the greatest mystery of all. *What had happened to Aiza?*

"You can't dwell on this forever," Stephanie said, perhaps sensing Sera's thoughts were still square on her sister. "You have a new family and we need you here with us."

"We?"

"Of course we. You're my sister now. Which reminds me, I brought something for you."

Sera had to blink rapidly to alleviate the new sting of tears. To gain a man like Seth as a lover, a protector, and a husband was a literal dream come true. Gaining a sister like Stephanie was like a balm on her heart.

Stephanie presented a small square box. Sera opened it slowly, gasping softly at the sight of the delicate gold and diamonds, shaped into the silhouette of a wolf. "Oh, it's beautiful. Is it an antique?"

"Yes, it's been passed down in our pack for generations."

"Oh, I can't accept this," Sera said, quickly replacing the broach in the box. She'd met several members of Seth's pack, and they'd all been kind to her, but she didn't consider herself to be worthy of receiving such an important gift. "You should keep it. It probably looks beautiful on you."

"It does, but I want you to have it and I'm sure Marian would have wanted that, too."

"Marian?"

"Yes. She was our Alpha. She mentored me. She is who prepared me to be an Alpha."

"All the more reason for you to keep it. To remember her by."

Stephanie pressed the box into Sera's palm. "I don't need this to remember her. If you don't want to keep it, please at least wear it tonight."

"I will wear it tonight with pride. Thank you." She accepted the box. "I can't believe it's happening tonight."

Stephanie smiled. "I'm so excited. Everyone is going to be there."

Sera almost corrected her. Not *everyone,* certainly. Obviously, she would feel Aiza's absence, but her parents had declined her invitation, and her brother said he wanted to be there, but with a toddler and another baby on the way, he was stretched thin these days.

"Is everything ready? Does Jackie need help with anything?"

"Jackie has everything under control," Stephanie assured her. "I don't want to jinx anything but—"

Sera held up her hand. "Then don't."

"Okay, I won't jinx it. I was just going to say that it'll be—"

"Don't jinx it!" Sera laughed. "So...the whole pack is going to be there?"

"Nearly."

"How many is that?"

"Around one hundred."

Sera whistled between her teeth. "That's a lot of people. How will I remember their names?"

"It's okay, you don't have to remember everyone's name tonight."

"What if they don't—"

"Don't what?"

"Like me," Sera said.

"Well, they don't *know* you. Once they do get to know you, they will like you. In the meantime, they all really love Seth. You make him happy, so they will adore you. He's been alone for a long time."

"How long?"

"Since...well, since he was eighteen."

"When you two became Alphas?"

"Yes."

"Why were you so young?" Sera inquired, giving in to her curiosity for the first time. "Didn't anyone challenge you?"

"There was nobody left to challenge us. Our pack was nearly destroyed. Once the fighting stopped, all that remained were the kids and seniors. We'd both been trained to lead the pack since birth; we just didn't count on starting so soon."

Sera's mouth dropped open. "All of the adults were killed?"

"Yes."

"By who?"

"The Wolf Brotherhood. It was a territory dispute. They wanted Portland and they got it."

"Sorry I'm late," Peggy said, bursting through the back door. "I'm dealing with a real bear of a client. Talk talk talk, blah blah blah...I'm parched. Mind if I get myself a drink? No, no honey, stay off your feet. I can pour my own water. Oh, I can't wait to see you in your dress. God, you're going to look gorgeous."

"I HATE TO BE THE BEARER OF BAD NEWS," NOAH SAID, gesturing to his Alpha to have a seat. Dana had offered to call Seth and tell him the news, but Noah had declined. Seth deserved to hear it from him, not from a stranger.

"I hate to hear it. But you'd better lay it on me anyway," Seth said, remaining on his feet.

"We just got a positive ID back on a John Doe. We had to use dental records and DNA and there's really no margin of error on this one." Noah took a deep breath. "It's Tony."

Seth rubbed his eyes with his thumb and forefinger, his face creased in a deep frown. Noah held his tongue, waiting for Seth to process the information. Only Noah knew how many times Seth had traveled to Portland in search of their lost pack mate. Noah's most fervent hope was that his own investigation wouldn't intersect with Seth's search, and yet, he'd prayed every day for a chance to give Seth and the rest of the pack a sense of closure.

"The Brotherhood?" Seth finally asked.

"We think so. I didn't want to give you this news today, of all days, but I thought you would like to know."

"They took his life and for what? Because he showed his face in Portland?"

"That's part of what I'm working on finding out," Noah said. "There were other remains we're working on ID-ing. If things go our way for once, we might have enough info to make some arrests.

"What do you mean?"

"I can't divulge much," Noah said, "but we have an eyewitness we're working with. If we can link any of the remains to her statement, we'll have enough to get a warrant."

"A warrant? Is that going to be enough to take out that viper's nest?"

"It'll be a start."

Noah could see that wasn't enough for Seth, and frankly, it wasn't enough for him, either. The only reason he joined H.O.W.L. was to take down the Wolf

Brotherhood once and for all. Every inroad he made met a dead-end and every lead he found met the same fate. He hoped finding Aiza Simpson and taking her into protective custody would change his luck, but so far, there was little to be optimistic about.

"I will find the sonsabitches responsible for this," Noah said, when he couldn't bear another second of Seth's frown or silence. "I won't give up until I do."

"I know you won't give up, Noah. But how many of us can they slaughter before somebody finally stops them? I mean, are you the only one here who cares?" Seth demanded.

"I'm definitely not the only one here who cares. There are a lot of good agents working on this case with me." As soon as Noah finished speaking, his phone erupted with Dana's personalized ringtone. "I've got to take this."

"I'll leave you to it." Seth stood and held out his hand. "I'll see you tonight?"

Noah shook his hand. "I wouldn't miss it for the world. I'm really excited to meet the woman who finally trapped the wolf." As soon as Seth stepped out of his office, Noah brought the phone to his ear. "Talk to me."

"It's Aiza."

"What about her? Is she hurt?"

"I don't think so. I don't know because she's not here, Noah." Dana's voice was calm, but he still caught the edge under her words.

"What do you mean? Did she go for a walk? Maybe she's at the grocery store."

"She's not here. She's not in town. She left a note saying she was going back to Portland."

"*What*?"

"I contacted her detail. They said she went to Paul's Tavern and now she's at The Eight Ball, across the street. There's been no suspicious activity but Pete said she's been in that bar for a long time."

"I'm heading there now."

"Keep in touch," Dana said before the call ended.

Noah would like to say that he was surprised by this development, but he was not in the least. Aiza had shown remarkable patience, given the situation, but even a blind man could see her advanced case of cabin fever. He did what he could to alleviate it, but he was really her only source of social contact; her only real link to the outside world. And he couldn't even visit her every day.

Even though he wanted to.

That had been a great surprise, the day he realized he was truly looking forward to the three-hour drive that would take him to Aiza. After that, there were dozens of smaller realizations, all of them genuinely unexpected. He liked the way she laughed, the way she smirked when she told a dirty joke, the way she got angry over books and weepy over stupid movies. He liked the way she downed whiskey, poured beer, and made cereal for dinner. He didn't even care if she talked to him, and sometimes she didn't have a single word to say to him past greetings and the formalities—he just liked spending time with her.

So far, he kept their interactions completely professional and appropriate, as though Dana was standing over his shoulder, monitoring every word. In a way, she was, since Aiza's entire safe house was wired with mics and cameras. Their hope had been that Aiza was much deeper in the pack than she initially let on, but her story never changed, and nobody in the gang sought her out. He was beginning to believe that her only connection to the Brotherhood was Dwight, and since he was dead, Noah wasn't certain what value Aiza would bring to their investigation.

But he still didn't want her wandering around Portland. The thought of anything happening to her made his blood boil and the vein in his temple throb. He told himself his concern was entirely professional, stemming from the fact that she was still a witness, after all, and she'd already been through so much.

Deep down inside, he knew the truth. He didn't want anything to happen to her because he would miss her. Because he cared about her.

He didn't keep to the speed limit on the drive to Portland, though it probably made no difference at all. She could be on her way back to the safe house —*if* she intended to return; *if* somebody didn't find her before he did. It occurred to him that if he *did* find her, she might refuse to leave with him. She wasn't under any legal obligation and there hadn't been any threats against her in the last five months; she might insist she was perfectly capable of living her own life.

When he finally reached Portland, he went directly to The Eight Ball. A text from Dana confirmed the men still had eyes on her there. The bar was dark and he had to wait a minute to let his eyes adjust before he finally located her, hunched in the back corner booth, hands wrapped loosely around a giant, nearly empty stein.

"Can I buy you a drink?" Noah asked.

She didn't look up. "They took it."

"They took what?"

"Everything. It's all theirs now. Like nothing I did in my life mattered at all."

"The bar?" Noah slid into the booth beside her. He wanted to take her hand, but kept a respectful distance between them.

"I missed it. I wanted to see it. I know I shouldn't have left but I couldn't stand seeing those fucking beige carpets for another second. I just wanted to see my bar, you know?"

"I understand. I wish you would have told me, though. We could have arranged something."

"Well, it doesn't matter anyway. You can tell those nice men to stop following me."

"What do you mean?"

"It doesn't matter. They're not coming after me again. They already have exactly what they wanted. Exactly what I handed over to them...like a fucking idiot."

"Hey." Now he did take her hand. "You are not a fucking idiot. You were manipulated and controlled and you know what happened to you? Theft by deception. And you know what we're going to do?"

"What?"

He squeezed her fingers. "We're going to get it all back."

"How?"

"Well, first thing's first. You've got to tell me everything that happened today."

"I'm going to need that drink you mentioned."

"Coming right up," Noah promised as he eased out of the booth. When he returned with a pitcher of beer and two fresh steins, she was listlessly picking at the bowl of peanuts, popping them into her mouth one at a time, her eyes staring, unseeing, into the middle distance.

"I used to suck at this," Noah said conversationally as he began to pour. "I bet you're really good at it."

"I guess so."

He slid the stein over and filled his before prompting her with a gentle, "So what happened?"

"I just wanted to walk by and see if it was still open. I didn't plan to go inside or even stop, but then I noticed Chad and Cyn outside on a smoke break and I...I had to talk to them." She looked up. "I know, we agreed they should continue to think I'm dead, but...well..."

"What did they say?" Noah prompted.

"At first they couldn't believe it was me. I told them that I had to pretend to be dead for my own protection. They told me that the bar never even closed for a day. They came to work and the new owner told them that I was dead and he was taking over. Everything was as fine and legal as you please. Their checks never stopped, so they thought everything was kosher. Until—" She paused there and took a long drink. Noah waited.

"Until the new owner, Adam, announced a new policy. He would collect and pool all the tips and pay them out at the end of the night. Only, he doesn't always remember to pay them. He's working them into the ground. Hell, it sounds like he's running the whole fucking *place* into the ground." She shook her head. "All of this bullshit to get the bar and they're going to destroy it."

"Did anybody see you speaking to them?"

"No...no, I don't think so."

"Did they give you the new owner's full name?"

"Adam Pettyjohn."

"And he's a member of the Wolf Brotherhood?"

"They said he wears the patch. And it would make sense, right? Dwight got everything when I 'died' and he implied that what's his is theirs."

"It does make sense," Noah agreed. "Given what we know about how the pack is structured."

"I don't know. Maybe I should just go."

"Go where?"

Aiza gestured vaguely. "Anywhere. Away from here. Maybe I should move to the desert."

"What about the bar?"

She shrugged. "What does it matter? It's already gone. I don't even know who I am anymore. And on top of that, I've lost my sister. So why stay? Maybe it's time to start my life over."

"All alone?"

"What other choice do I have?"

"You could stay here," Noah suggested. "You can help me bring down the gang and get your bar back. And..." He took a deep breath. "You could see your sister again."

"My sister?" She looked up sharply. "What do you know about her?"

"I know where she is. I know she's doing well. She's happy."

"I want to see her," Aiza said immediately. "I need to see her. I need to tell her what happened." She took his hand, squeezing it fervently. "Please."

"Yes, of course. I can arrange that. Maybe in a few weeks or a month."

"Weeks? Months?" Aiza shook her head. "No. I need to see her now. Today."

"Today?"

"Yes. If I can see her today, I'll go back to the safe

house with those damned beige carpets and I won't complain and I'll stay as long as you need me to."

Noah had the sense to know that the timing of the request was absolutely awful, but no matter how he sought for the strength to deny her, he couldn't find it within himself to tell her no.

"She's a few hours from here with my cousin," Noah said. "We'd better hit the road."

"Oh my God, thank you!" She flung her arms around him in an exuberant hug, a smile lighting her face for the first time in ages. "I just need a chance to make this right."

Noah returned the hug, taking a deep breath and absorbing her scent, enjoying the warmth passing between them. Contact between them was always casual, brief and incidental, after their first night, when she hugged him without shame, seeking comfort. He'd relived that embrace in his dreams over and over, never expecting more than that.

"Let's go," she said, pulling away to wiggle from the booth. The life had returned to her eyes and there was even an extra bounce in her step. If he had any second thoughts, they were banished by the sight of her excitement.

7

As soon as the Fed and the bitch drove out of sight, Braxton hurried down the street to Paul's Tavern, slipping through the service door and directly to the back office. He didn't bother knocking on the door, as he was on orders to return as quickly as possible with any pertinent updates. Adam was sitting at the desk, staring at his computer screen with a small frown. One of the most senior members of the Wolf Brotherhood, he looked almost out of place behind the massive monitor.

"Sir?"

"What is it?" Adam's voice was rough, his throat all sand and gravel. "I thought I told you to stick with that bitch!"

"She left. With the Fed."

"What? Where did they go?"

"I don't know."

Adam looked up, his frown deepening as his eyes narrowed. "What do you mean you don't know? Why didn't you follow them?"

"I..."

"I told you to stick with her," Adam growled.

Braxton shrank back, a shiver of fear rolling down his spine. "I don't have a car."

"Well that's just great. Now we know fuck-all about where she's been hiding, what she knows, or what she's already told the feds." He shook his head. "This is why I don't like loose ends. Did you at least overhear anything?"

"Yes. They're going to see her sister."

"Her sister? I meant anything helpful, you idiot."

"Her sister is with Seth Longtail."

Adam's face changed slightly. He didn't exactly smile but his frown wasn't quite so severe. "Longtail, you say. They're going now?"

"Yes."

"The Longtails are still up in Washington," Adam said to himself, then lapsed into a long silence. Braxton waited patiently, remaining perfectly still and silent while his boss worked through his thoughts. "The Fed is a Longtail, too, isn't he?"

"Yes, sir."

"I don't think any of this is a coincidence. We should have killed that girl when we had the chance." He tapped his fingers against the desk and then nodded. "I want you to take Chuck and head on up to Yakima. Don't stop searching until you find both of those Simpson bitches and bring them back here."

"The Longtails might not let them go without a fight," Braxton said, a little uneasily. He'd already crossed paths with Seth Longtail and lived to tell about it. He didn't want to press his luck with a second meeting.

"Then give them a fight. We should have wiped them all out when we had the chance, anyway."

"Then maybe we should bring Don and Dave with us for reinforcements?"

Adam waved his hand dismissively. "Take whoever you want. Just get your asses moving."

"Yes, sir."

"Now, pup!" Adam roared.

Braxton jumped and hurried out the door, the hair on the back of his neck standing on end. He found Chuck, Don, and Dave sitting at the bar, taking turns making lewd comments at Cynthia and downing beers on the house. None of them wanted to leave their comfortable spots, but when Braxton told them it was on Adam's orders, they all jumped to their feet with shifty looks, as though they expected their boss heard their bitching and grumbling.

"Where are we going?" Chuck asked.

"Yakima."

"What the fuck is in Yakima?" Don wanted to know.

"Loose ends. Let's get moving."

8

THE BUTTERFLIES IN SERA'S STOMACH DOUBLED WITH every passing minute, until it felt like she was going to choke on her own excitement. It was so hard to believe that all of this was really happening. Every time she looked in the mirror, she barely recognized the woman staring back—and that was doubly true today. The woman in the mirror looked so happy, so beautiful, skin and eyes glowing.

She turned to the side, smoothing her hand over her stomach. For the moment, the baby was sleeping, and the dress laid flat against her skin. She'd gained weight with the pregnancy, but she didn't feel self-conscious or uneasy about that. The dress itself was very flattering for her full figure, emphasizing her bust with a sweetheart neckline and hiding the bulge of her stomach behind an empire waist and full skirt.

A sudden, sharp pain low in her belly distracted her from the dress. She nearly doubled over, her breath quickening as she tried to ride out the pain. *Probably just a cramp,* she thought. Strange pains and moments of discomfort were just a common part of her life now, and she did her best to ignore them and push through without complaint. Still, she couldn't completely shake her uneasiness. That was the fifth pain like that since that morning, and it was only getting sharper.

She moved away from the mirror to sit on the edge of the bed and took a long drink of water from her chilled bottle. Stephanie was downstairs, directing the last-minute moves and changes. From outside, she could hear the shouts and laughter of children playing while their parents finished setting everything up. A breeze wafted through the open window, bringing with it the smell of roast pork. They'd buried a whole pig in the ground with hot coals twenty-four hours earlier, and now it was done and ready to be feasted on.

Of course, there wasn't just pork. Sera's eyes had widened and nearly popped out of her head when Stephanie had detailed everything that would be prepared for the bonding ceremony. Chicken and duck, beef heart and liver, pounds of seafood brought in fresh from the coast, a half dozen different types of salads, fresh vegetables, potatoes prepared three ways, and God knows what else. When Sera had ventured to ask what all of this cost, Seth waved away her question with a smile. "You don't need to worry about that. You don't need to worry about anything."

Feeling a little better after her break, Sera crossed the room to the window and watched a half-dozen pack members run around, setting up chairs, hanging decorations, putting together the final touches. There were two huge wooden structures on either end of the yard. They looked like teepees without the tent. Once the sun went down, both would be lit into massive bonfires. Decorative citronella candles were being lit one by one to keep all the mosquitoes under control during the sunset ceremony, and the round tables were being set and prepared for the feast.

And all of it, every bit of it, was for her.

It was so hard to believe that this was her actual, real life and not a dream she was having between one lonely day and the next.

And yet, she couldn't quite be happy. She

couldn't quite summon a real smile to her lips. Talking over everything with Stephanie had done nothing to dull the pain and regret she felt over Aiza.

Another sharp pain drove her to the nearest chair. She winced and sat down, absently rubbing the spot that kept causing her so much trouble. "What's going on in there, baby? Are you excited about the big night, too?"

Excited or not, the pain was not abating this time. She tried to reach for her bottle of water, but another sudden, sharp cramp overtook her, and her fingers stiffened, knocking the bottle to the floor.

She reached for it without thinking, and another cramp nearly made her double over. She gasped for breath, trying to remember the Lamaze exercises from her the class, but the pain overwhelmed her. She couldn't think, couldn't catch her breath, and couldn't even shout for help as the waves rolled through her, growing more intense by the second.

It felt like an eternity passed before the pain faded enough for her to think. She abandoned the bottle of water on the floor and began searching for her phone. She finally caught sight of it on the other side of the room, sitting on the corner of the nightstand. With a low groan, she forced herself to her feet—a necessary motion, but it proved to be a very bad idea as another tsunami of pain ripped through her.

With a groan, she forced herself to take a step and then another. It felt like she was walking through thick quicksand, like the floor itself was grasping at her ankles and holding her in place. It was then she felt something thick and warm flowing down her thighs. Fear stabbed through her and she closed her eyes, trying to focus, trying not to lose herself completely to pain and panic. When she opened her eyes again, there was a drop of blood on the floor between her feet. That drop was quickly joined by another and then another.

She shuffled the remaining distance, reaching blindly for the phone. Seth's number was at the top of her contact list. She automatically called him first, but the phone rang with no answer until the voice-mail picked up.

"It's me. There's something wrong. I need help." She hung up the call and blindly stabbed at the next number on the list. The phone rang twice before Stephanie answered.

"Hey, what do you need?"

"Help," Sera croaked out. The blood no longer came in drops. "I'm bleeding."

"What? I'll be right there! Jackie! Call an ambulance!"

"Where's...Seth?" Sera gasped out.

"I'll get him. Don't worry about that. Don't move. There's an ambulance on its way."

"Hurry," Sera mumbled before the phone fell from her fingers. She didn't try to pick it up. Her knees buckled and she leaned heavily to the side, bracing herself against the mattress. Unable to stay on her feet for another second, she sank to her knees. At that point, she must have blacked out, because the next thing she was aware of was Stephanie's voice.

"Go find Seth. He's not answering his phone. Where's that ambulance?"

"I can hear the sirens!" someone called out.

"Go down and meet them. Sera? Sera can you hear me?"

"It hurts," Sera moaned. "Where's Seth?"

"He's coming," Stephanie promised. "He'll be here any second."

"There's...there's something wrong..." Sera sobbed from another sharp pain. "I need Seth."

"He'll be here. He'll be—"

"Okay, everybody, clear out."

Sera barely noticed the arrival of the EMTs. She

sensed the flurry of activity around her; she felt them take her pulse and heard one of them say her name, but it was all happening very far away from her, and she couldn't even register it. They lifted her onto a stretcher, holding her to it as a cramp wracked her body with agony. When she came back to herself, they were already outside of the cabin, hurrying towards the ambulance.

"Where am I going?" she gasped out. "Where are you taking me? Seth? Stephanie?"

"Can I ride with her?"

The EMTs lifted Sera into the ambulance and Stephanie climbed in after her, taking Sera's hand in hers.

"Where's Seth?" Sera mumbled.

"He'll meet us there."

That was the last thing Sera heard before she slipped away from the pain and into the welcoming darkness.

9

AIZA AND NOAH PULLED INTO THE PACKED DRIVEWAY just as the ambulance pulled away. Aiza was reaching for the door before the car had even stopped moving, but Noah put a hand on her arm, holding her in place.

"Sit tight while I find out what's going on."

"But—"

"Please, Aiza."

She nodded, sinking back into the seat. He gave her a small smile and then jumped out of the car, hurrying across the yard to the nearest person, a woman who looked about the same age as Noah and had the same coloring in her hair and eyes. They only spoke for a few moments. Aiza noticed the woman pointing at the ambulance down the road, and then Noah hurried back to the car.

"It's Sera. They're taking her to the hospital. It might be the baby."

Aiza's eyes widened. "*Baby?* Sera's pregnant?"

"Yes." Noah put the car in reverse and flew down the driveway back to the narrow road. Aiza braced herself as he stepped on the accelerator, racing to catch up with the ambulance.

"What happened? Did she fall? Did somebody hurt her?"

Noah shook his head. "Nobody knows what happened. She was bleeding and cramping. That's all Jess knew."

"Oh my God. Oh my God, I can't believe this is happening!"

"I'm sure everything's going to be fine."

"No you're not," Aiza shot back. "You can't possibly know that everything's going to be fine. She could be...what if something happens to her...I never even had the chance to apologize."

Noah's only answer was to push harder on the gas pedal, closing the distance between them and the ambulance. The nearest hospital was almost thirty miles away, and Aiza passed every mile in greater agony, her heart sick and strained with fear for her baby sister. *Pregnant. How could she be pregnant?*

The wolf she'd been with must have been the father. Most of the events of that terrible night were gone from her memory, but she did recall fighting that man and trying to kill him. He had fought hard, and though Aiza was strong, the man had been stronger—and yet, he hadn't killed her. Of course, there was no guarantee he wouldn't kill her if he saw her again. Hopefully, Noah wouldn't let that happen.

The sudden ringing from his phone pulled Aiza from her thoughts, her heart inexplicably jumping to her throat. He punched the Bluetooth button on his dash. "Seth, where are you?"

Seth's voice filled the cabin, flowing from the stereo speakers. "I have a flat tire, about ten miles from the cabin."

"Have you talked to anybody?"

"No, I'm in a dead spot. This is the first call I could get through."

"Where are you? I'll be right there."

Seth named the location and Noah promised to be there within five minutes. Aiza silently watched him drive, noting the thin compression of his lips and the white-knuckled grip on the wheel. The ambulance was out of sight, and she couldn't hear the sirens either. *Go to the hospital. Send somebody else to get him. Who cares about this guy? My sister is in danger.*

Noah pushed the accelerator, eyes narrowed against the sun. He took a sharp right turn and then another left, and nerves crawled through Aiza's stomach and up her throat. Each second was an eternity, increasing the certainty that she would never see her sister; that she was too late, and this stupid detour would only prolong the inevitable. Her nerves turned to sharp, undeniable fear when the car and man finally came into sight.

"Oh my God," she gasped.

"What?"

"That's *him.*"

"Who?"

"The one with Sera. The one I nearly....I tried to...I attacked him."

"That's...don't worry about that."

He pulled to a stop behind Seth's car and hopped out of the vehicle. She heard Seth say something about the proper tools, but Noah shook his head and took Seth by the elbow, leading him to the car. The good-natured smile disappeared from Seth's face, and a storm gathered between the creases of his brow.

"How long ago?" Aiza heard his question distinctly.

"Just a few minutes before you called me. Come on." He opened the back door and helped Seth inside. Aiza sank lower in her seat, trying to obscure her features. Not that he was paying any attention to her. His anxiety was palpable, and as soon as Noah slid behind the wheel, he had a thousand questions. But Noah had no answers. Except for the last one.

"Who's this?" Seth finally asked.

"This is Aiza Simpson," Noah said.

"*What?*"

"Now don't get angry, Seth."

"Don't get angry? I have every right to get angry. She tried to kill us. She tried to kill *Sera*. And you bring her here? What the fuck were you thinking?" Seth's voice got louder with each syllable, the final question coming out as a roar. Aiza automatically flinched away, trying to make herself smaller against the door, eyes darting back and forth from Noah to Seth.

"She's under my protection, Seth, and she's cooperating in the investigation against the Wolf Brotherhood. She's not any danger to you or to Sera."

"How do you know that?"

"Because I know her, Seth. Far better than you do."

"She faked her own death and tried to murder her own sister," Seth said harshly. "I know enough. You can't trust her."

Aiza winced and swallowed the sudden lump in her throat. Of course he would see her this way. He didn't know any better and had no reason to believe that she was truly a different person. His reaction was perfectly normal and perfectly expected, and it was probably exactly what she should expect from Sera, too.

Oh God, Sera.

"I trust her," Noah said, his voice as even and calm as before, a sharp contrast to Seth's anger. "She was under the power of her maker wolf, and she wasn't acting on her own wishes. She was violated, Seth, and now she's helping me stop the wolves who hurt her." He glanced up, meeting Seth's eyes in the rearview mirror. "The wolves who hurt *us*."

"Why did you bring her here?" Seth's voice was calmer but he was far from placated.

"I made her a deal. She wanted to see her sister."

"But today, Noah? Of all days? Did Sera see her? Is that why—"

"No. The ambulance was already leaving as we

arrived."

"What's today?" Aiza asked softly.

"Our wedding day."

"Oh." Aiza's head was spinning with the news. Sera was pregnant. Sera was getting married. Sera was starting a new life with a man who clearly loved her. Why had Noah agreed to bring Aiza on that day of all days? And why did she think she had any right to disrupt her sister's life after everything she put Sera through?

Nobody spoke again until they reached the hospital. Seth jumped out of the car almost before it stopped moving, racing through the double doors of the emergency room.

"Maybe this isn't a good idea," Aiza muttered.

"I think Sera needs her family."

"She has her family. Her *new* family. And she's probably much better off with them."

"Yeah, but they're not blood. You know, Seth told me nobody came for her. Not her parents or her brother. Not even any friends."

AIZA'S HEART TWISTED, but her stomach was still in knots of fear, tightened by self-doubt.

"Come on. You don't want to miss out on this

chance. Trust me."

"What if he doesn't let me see her?" Aiza asked.

"He'll let you see her. Seth is a good man, Aiza. He's a good wolf and a good Alpha. And he loves your sister so goddamned much he'll do anything to make her happy." He said the words with such open and simple sincerity that she couldn't doubt him. "Do you trust me?"

"You're the only one in this world I do trust," Aiza admitted.

"Come on then."

Other members of the Longtail pack had followed the ambulance, and since they weren't slowed down by an unexpected detour, they were already in the ER waiting room, staring anxiously at Seth, who was caught in a low conversation with a doctor. Noah led Aiza to the nearest chair, seating himself between her and the rest of the family, a protective hand on her arm. She felt the curious eyes fall on her, and she wondered how much they all knew about her and her last, unfortunate encounter with Seth and Sera.

"She's in emergency surgery," Seth said to no one in particular and everyone at once after the doctor walked away. "She's lost a lot of blood. She may...they don't know...about the baby."

Seth's pack immediately surrounded him, offering hugs and encouraging words and comfort. Aiza remained rooted to her chair, Noah at her side. The weight of his hand on her arm was the only sense of comfort she had, and it was fleeting. She wanted more. She wanted to curl herself against his chest and let his strong arms hold her there until this nightmare was finally over. She wanted him to stroke her hair and tell her everything would be all right, and then take her home and continue to hold her until she fell asleep. She wanted a hug.

But she didn't deserve any of it, and so she remained as still and cold as a marble statue, the tears frozen behind her eyes.

It was impossible to say how much time passed before the same doctor emerged from behind the closed doors and gestured for Seth. He only said a few words before Seth broke away and ran past the orderlies, disappearing behind the swinging doors.

"Sir! You can't go back there! Security!"

The waiting room suddenly erupted with noise and confusion. It quickly became clear to Aiza that the pack, far from helping the security guards and orderlies, was trying to stop them and create extra chaos to buy their Alpha some time. Nobody noticed Aiza in the general melee, and she took the opportunity to slip away from Noah and rush after Seth, using her nose to track his path.

He led her right to Sera's bed. She looked so pale and helpless against the hospital sheets, with all kinds of wires and tubes protruding from her limp body. Aiza's eyes flew to the monitors, which still showed a heartbeat and oxygen levels, but all the numbers seemed much too low.

"Let go of me," Seth shouted, wrenching his arm away from a nurse that was trying to hold him back from the bed. "She's *dying!*"

"Sir, sir, you have to calm down. We can help her, but—"

"You *can't* help her. She's dying right now. And I'm not going to let that happen."

Aiza understood, better than anybody, what Seth intended to do, but everything was moving in slow motion. She tried to reach for him, but she was too far away and grabbed nothing but air. She opened her mouth, trying to beg him not to do it, not to curse Sera the way she was cursed, but all that escaped was a whimper. His face shifted, his mouth elongating into a snout, his teeth descending into sharp, brutal points. One of the nurses screamed, and Aiza hoped that would be enough to distract him. But he didn't even seem to notice it.

"Don't," she choked out.

Seth looked up, his eyes twin discs of silver. "I can't let her die."

Aiza had nothing to say to that. She could do nothing, think of nothing except the reality of never seeing her sister again. Seth opened his mouth, his teeth flashing under the fluorescent lights, and then sank his fangs into the fleshy skin above Sera's elbow.

Sera's eyes flew open as soon as his jaw closed, and she looked directly at Aiza. First there was fear, then confusion—and then a flash of pain that Aiza felt in the center of her own heart.

"I'm sorry," Aiza whispered, as the wolf's virus entered her sister's bloodstream. The change was immediate. Her heart rate increased, as did her blood pressure. Color returned to her cheeks and Sera had enough strength to scream.

"He's coming! Oh God, oh God, the baby. He's coming!"

One doctor went to the foot of her bed while another nurse finally pulled Seth away from her. Seth didn't resist the nurse, but stood watching with a bloody mouth and wild eyes as his son kicked, screamed, and clawed his way into the world.

10

Noah managed to drag Aiza out of the emergency department and back to his car before they put the entire hospital on lockdown, which was the standard protocol when dealing with werewolf attacks. Hospital security had swarmed around Seth, dragging him to the ground and forcing his hands behind his back, though he did nothing to resist them, his attention locked on Sera's still face. The nurses moved with the precision of an ant colony, working around the chaos to see to the baby and new mother. A voice overhead warned the staff that they were in the middle of a code 9653, and all patients were to remain in their rooms until further notice.

Aiza barely even noticed the pressure of Noah's

hand on her arm or the way he shoved her into the front seat. She was too dazed, too absorbed by Sera. She wanted to go back to her sister—wanted to protect her from further attack and to hold her hand —but she knew that wasn't an option. Not with the security staff in the hospital on full alert and the cops on their way.

"What's going to happen?" Aiza asked as Noah put the car into gear. "Why aren't we staying?"

"Trust me. You don't want to get caught up in this shitshow."

"But what about Sera? Is she going to be okay? Is Seth going to be arrested?"

"She'll probably be okay and he probably won't be arrested."

"What if he *is* arrested? Can't you help him?"

Noah shook his head. "Not my jurisdiction. The cops might arrest him tonight, but unless Sera wants to make a statement and press charges, he won't be going to jail."

"Well, if everything's going to be okay, why are we running?"

"I never said everything's going to be okay," Noah pointed out. "At any rate, the Brotherhood has eyes and ears everywhere. Literally, everywhere. All it takes is one asshole and your cover is blown."

"My sister just had a baby and was turned into a werewolf and you're telling me I can't be with her?"

"For now. Look, Aiza, I'm sorry. Believe me, this was not my first choice. But your safety is my number one priority, and I couldn't risk you being exposed."

"Where are we going?"

Noah frowned. "It's too far to make it to the safe house tonight. I need to go back to Seth's and give everybody an update, then we'll find a hotel."

As Aiza did not want to return to the safe house at all, she signaled her agreement with a nod and turned her attention to the perfect darkness outside the window. The moon wasn't visible through the blanket of clouds, and once they left the town limits behind, there were no streetlights or even oncoming headlights to break through the void.

"Is she going to be okay?" Aiza asked, without turning to face him. "Is it...is the bite going to fix her like it fixed me?"

"I reckon it should."

"And is she...Seth wouldn't hurt her, would he?"

"Aiza, I trust Seth with my life. I trust him with the lives of my family. If you're worried he'll try to control her, don't be. As an alpha, he has that power over every wolf in his pack, and he's never used it."

"Well, not to your knowledge. I just don't want her to go through what I've been through."

"Aiza, do you trust me?"

She opened her mouth to give an automatic *of course I trust you*, but the words were stuck on the back of her tongue. She *did* trust him. She truly believed he meant to help her, that he had no intention of causing her arm, and that he was a good man. In fact, she would go as far as to say he was the best man she'd ever met. Honest, kind, patient, intelligent, and dedicated.

"I'm...I'm sorry."

"Don't be sorry," Noah said softly.

"But I *am* sorry. You've never given me a single reason not to trust you but I just...I can't..."

"You can't trust anybody, or anything, right now. I know. You can't trust yourself. You can't trust the law. You can't trust the wolf who took your sister. You can't trust your only friend. And I'm not going to ask you to because you have a very good reason to be on your guard. But I am asking you to recognize that your experiences have shaped the lens you use to view the world."

"Are you telling me that everywhere I look, I see Dwight?"

"Can you tell me that's not the case?"

"No," Aiza admitted softly. "He's...he's everywhere. Sometimes I'm so scared he's still in my brain and wonder if I'm making choices of my own free will, or if I'm still responding to his programming on some level. I think I still dream about him."

"He's not in control of you anymore."

"How do you know?" Aiza demanded.

"Have you harmed anybody? Have you killed anybody? Have you wronged anybody?"

"No, but maybe it's because I haven't had the chance."

"You just watched Seth bite your sister," Noah pointed out, his voice low and even. "You didn't attack him. You could have turned and lunged for his throat in a blink of an eye. Nobody would have been able to stop you. But you didn't do it. It didn't even occur to you, did it?"

It hadn't occurred to her, but Aiza didn't know if that necessarily meant anything. She hadn't shifted once since the night she nearly killed Sera, and she had no intention of ever shifting again. She wished she could have the wolf removed completely. And now her system was burdened with the same beast. Was it so hard to imagine that one day she would be burdened by the same fears? The same guilt and recrimination?

"I want to see her in the morning. I'll need to see her."

"I'll do my best to make that happen."

It wasn't the answer she wanted, but she would accept it because she did trust him that far. He would do his best.

He slowed, turning onto the narrow, unpaved road that led to Seth's home. Something in the air changed and her nose trembled as the sleeping wolf inside of her began to stir.

"What's that?"

"It's blood," Noah said grimly, pressing on the accelerator, though he couldn't gain much speed on the loose gravel.

Her first thought was that maybe the scent of Sera's blood had lingered in the air, but it was too strong. Too fresh. Her heart jumped to her throat while her stomach dropped to her knees, and in the sudden yawning gulf between them, she felt nothing but dread, dark and sludgy. She tried to brace herself, but she still didn't know how to prepare herself for the worst.

The yard surrounding Seth's cabin was full of vehicles and all windows glowed with light—and yet, there was no noise. Noah killed the engine and they sat for a beat in the heavy silence before throwing open the car doors and racing towards the house, the smell of blood growing stronger and stronger with each step.

"Stick with me," Noah instructed as he pushed the cabin's door open. They were met by more of that eerie silence. Aiza stayed close to Noah's heels, scanning the empty rooms for clues. Somebody had been there, and recently, too, judging by the state of the kitchen: the stove was still on, and half-prepared food waited for the return of the missing chef. A TV was on in the den, though the sound was off, and muddy boot prints led into the house from the back door, but not out again.

They paused at the back door, the stench of blood so overpowering that Aiza nearly gagged. She no longer felt dread, just a terrible certainty—one she didn't want to see confirmed. She reached out for Noah, putting a hand on his arm. He wrapped his fingers around hers and gave them a brief squeeze.

"Stay here. There might be…just…stay here."

He braced his foot against the wall and pulled his pant leg up, revealing a holster strapped to his shin. He pulled the pistol free and turned off the safety, sparing her another quick look before opening the door. She did as he instructed and stayed within the cabin as he took his first steps out, his gun at the ready.

"Aiza, there's a switch on the wall. Turn it on, please."

She did as he instructed, and light flooded the empty backyard. Aiza took her first easy breath since they reached the cabin. Still, the smell of blood was strong.

"Hello? Is there anybody here?" Noah's voice echoed through the dark trees.

A wolf melted from the shadows, shifting into a tall blond woman as she crossed the yard. Aiza found her familiar, though she couldn't recall her name or where they met. "Noah?"

"Stephanie? What happened here? Where is everybody?"

"We were attacked."

"By who?"

"The Brotherhood, I think. There were only four of them. I've got everybody in the panic room."

"Was anybody hurt?"

"A few bites and scratches, but nothing fatal."

"What about the attackers?"

Stephanie pointed to her nose and then gestured at the deep forest.

"You should get to the panic room, too," Noah said.

"You don't give the orders here, Noah."

Noah immediately looked chagrined. "I'm sorry but, I just meant it'll be safer there until the police arrive."

"They'll be long gone by then. I'm getting them, with or without your help."

"I'll help," Aiza said, before she realized she meant to speak at all.

Their heads whipped around and it was easy to see the family resemblance in their coloring and the way their eyes narrowed.

"What are you—" She looked back to Noah. "What the hell is *she* doing here?"

"I brought her—"

"*You* brought her? What the hell were you thinking?" Her words were low, her fury undeniable. And that was when Aiza realized why the woman seemed so familiar.

"That wasn't me," Aiza said quickly. "I mean, it was. It was me. But it wasn't—I didn't mean to do those things."

"She was under her maker's control," Noah said.

"Dwight?"

Noah nodded.

"That asshole was a real piece of work." Stephanie looked her up and down and then nodded. "Just try to keep up."

"Wait—" Noah started, but the withering look Stephanie gave him was enough to close his mouth.

"As I said, I'm going with or without you. It's entirely up to you if you want to come along."

"I'll go with you," Noah said.

"Stick with me. I don't want either one of you wandering off on your own."

Aiza undressed while Stephanie spoke and didn't think twice before shifting into her wolf form, despite her previous misgivings. She owed it to Stephanie to help her. She owed it to the Brotherhood to fight them. She owed it to herself to do the right thing.

Noah shifted beside her, and his scent changed as the wolf emerged. Aiza took a deep breath of it and barely contained her urge to bay at the moon. The fur on the back of her neck and tail stood on end, and she felt as though the air itself was electric. Her muscles tensed, and though her attention was on Stephanie, her senses were completely keyed into Noah's—she wanted to run with him; to hunt with him.

Stephanie darted forward and Aiza was right on

her heels, her body low to the ground, her ears laid back against her head. Noah was right behind her, so close she could feel his breath on her tail. Aiza had spent time with Dwight as a wolf, but only him. She had no idea what it felt like to hunt in a pack, no idea what was expected of her, and no idea of what she might be capable of if she had allies at her back. But it still felt natural to move with them, to follow Stephanie's lead as she took deep breaths, searching for that tendril of a scent.

There. She stopped, her tail and ears going up as her nostrils flared. Stephanie must have caught the same scent, because she changed direction without stopping, her steps so quick and light she made no sound at all, gliding through the underbrush like a ghost.

They came to a clearing, slinking on their stomachs to the edge of the shadow. Enough moonlight broke through the clouds to illuminate three men standing over a wolf. Its ragged breathing indicated that while it was still alive, it wouldn't be for long. Stephanie's ears went back, her lip curled in a silent snarl, and Aiza's response was bone deep, her body coiling, ready to spring forward in an instant.

She thought Noah was at her side, but she didn't

look to find out—not wanting to take her full attention from her alpha's target.

A cloud drifted over the moon, cloaking the figures in darkness, and that's when Stephanie made her move. She moved so swiftly that she had the target on the ground before anybody, including Aiza, knew she had moved at all. The two remaining men instantly transformed into the stronger, faster versions of themselves, giving Aiza the precious seconds she needed to put herself between them and Stephanie's vicious attacks.

Aiza remained in a defensive posture, primarily concerned with protecting Stephanie from attack. She snapped and snarled, aiming for the sensitive nose with each gnash of her teeth. Behind her, Stephanie's growls were now echoed as the target shifted as well. The subsequent fight was short and brutal, leaving the Brotherhood wolf maimed and whimpering on the ground.

As soon as that wolf was disposed of, Stephanie spun around and attacked the two wolves Aiza barely held at bay. The two wolves were young and fast, uninjured and furious at the attack. Their fighting style was fierce and vicious, and Aiza already felt herself tiring. But she didn't cede a single inch of ground, wheeling around and biting, lunging for flesh at every new aggression against Stephanie.

There was no way of knowing how long the fight lasted before a sudden gunshot drove the wolves apart. Aiza spun around, ready to attack the new threat, but she recognized Noah's scent through the blood and sulphur. The familiar scent stopped Stephanie as well, and the Brotherhood wolves took advantage of their distraction, but another loud blast from the gun put a stop to the attack.

The wolf fell just short of Aiza, his intended target, and the remaining wolf turned to bolt for the underbrush. Stephanie sprang through the air and landed on its back, her teeth sinking into his neck.

"Stephanie, stop!" Noah's voice echoed off the trees. At first, it seemed like Stephanie didn't hear him—or didn't care—but then her grip loosened. The wolf below her didn't move as she released him, but Aiza could still hear the sound of his breathing.

"We have to bring these men in."

Stephanie shifted immediately, her face twisted with fury and Aiza whined and sank to the ground.

"That's not your decision to make."

"It *is* my decision to make, Stephanie. You're my alpha, but this is my job. All of them are still alive and they're all going into custody tonight."

"So they can be released in the morning?" Stephanie scoffed. "All they have to do is make bail."

"Not this time," Noah said grimly. "This time, they made a very serious mistake. Help me get them to the car."

The entire time they spoke, Aiza remained on her stomach. The words meant very little to her, but the anger she sensed from the one she recognized as alpha made her stomach tight.

"What's wrong with her?" Stephanie asked. "Why hasn't she shifted back?"

Noah immediately dropped to one knee, running his fingers over her ribs and legs, searching for any damage. She turned her head and licked his hand with appreciation, and he cupped the side of her face. "Well, she's not hurt, but I'm guessing she wants to remain in wolf form for a while."

"She's pretty new then, huh?"

"Less than a year. You remember what it was like to be a young pup; let her enjoy herself."

"Alright, well, we need to get moving, so I'll go get the car. There's a road just a few hundred feet to the east," Stephanie said. "Aiza can stay here with you and help keep an eye on the prisoners."

"Yes, ma'am."

Stephanie shifted and trotted towards the trees.

Aiza made a move to follow, but Noah put a restraining hand on her neck, and she settled back at his feet.

"Well, let's get them all restrained before they wake up," Noah said, moving to the first prone figure. Aiza stayed at his side, moving in time with him like a shadow. Without any handcuffs, he had to improvise, using their discarded clothes to fashion ropes for their hands and feet, and to make bandages as needed. When they stirred, Aiza growled and snapped until they were still again.

Stephanie returned with someone's SUV and they moved the men one at a time, loading them into the vehicle. Throughout the process and the drive back to town, Aiza was relieved to let her human form slip away for a while.

To forget herself in the wolf.

11

By the time Noah made it back to his apartment, with Aiza the wolf in tow, he was utterly exhausted. He would have fallen directly in bed and gone right to sleep if it wasn't for the hollow ache in his stomach. Even if he could ignore the pain, the rumbling growls from his midsection would have kept him awake. So he bypassed the bed in favor of the fridge, finding a pound of hamburger and a few strips of bacon.

He shredded a strip of bacon and mixed it with half of the hamburger and an egg in a bowl, then placed it before Aiza. She quickly gobbled it up, and he took advantage of her distraction to do a more thorough check for injuries. He was concerned he missed something in the dark, though she hadn't shown any signs of being injured or lost any blood. She was definitely unhurt and in good shape, and his unmitigated relief almost knocked the strength from his legs.

As soon as the fight started, Noah shifted and pulled another hidden gun from a holster higher up, on his thigh. Once he joined H.O.W.L., he became very adept at strapping weapons to strategic places so he could shift without losing his gun in the process. He'd paused a moment before firing the first shot, entranced by the sight of his alpha and his —well, what *was* she to him?

A witness. That's all she can be. That's what Dana would say if he asked her. And she would be right, of course. The lines between them were already blurring enough without him adding any further complications, and yet, that didn't seem like the entire truth. Yes, she was an important witness, a key part to the case he was building, but he couldn't escape the fact that he was fond of her. He couldn't deny how happy it made him when she fell into step with his alpha, as though she were a part of his pack.

As though she were his.

Of course, she wanted to kill his other alpha, the man who had been at times a brother, a father, an alpha, and a friend. But there were obviously a lot of very intense feelings involved in that situation, and Noah was confident that once everyone had a chance to talk and reconcile, she would be as accepting of him as she was of Stephanie.

Which only mattered if Aiza would join the pack.

These thoughts ran around his head while he fried the hamburger and a few eggs. He ate quickly, chewing mechanically until his stomach was finally soothed. He brushed his teeth, stripped to his boxers and a T-shirt, and crawled into bed. Aiza watched with alert eyes, and jumped up to join him on the mattress, curling against his side.

He sighed and stroked the soft fur between her eyes. She would change back to her human form sooner or later. He knew exactly what it was like to give in to the wolf; to remain yourself and yet *other*. To know what it was to be yourself without the burden of guilt or the knowledge of fear. In her lycanthrope state, she was pure, her only concerns only of the most basic variety: food, shelter, and pack. At the moment, all of her needs were met and she could be perfectly satisfied. Perfectly at peace. She seemed content to sleep at his side, and he was more than happy to let her.

Even the call of much needed slumber couldn't

pull him away from her; Noah watched her sleep with heavy-lidded, gritty eyes. He had a big day ahead of him. All four of the attackers would live, and all were under heavy guard as they recovered in the hospital. Tomorrow he and Dana would work on breaking them down until they had enough for a warrant. And after that, he would finally have the Wolf Brotherhood right where he wanted them. Right in the center of his sights.

All of that could wait for the light of morning, though. It was so nice to run his fingers through her fur and over her ears, along the side of her snout and over her long leg. He felt his own relief at being able to offer her a moment of comfort, and he wanted to extend that moment for as long as possible. It was the first time he'd seen her at peace since he met her —and the first time he could take a breath and acknowledge his changing reality.

She nuzzled closer to his leg in her sleep, her body radiating heat. Normally, that would drive him crazy; now he just found it comforting. He called forth the wolf, not enough to shift his form, but enough to amplify his senses. His sharp ears told him they were safe, and his nose imprinted the scent of his sleeping mate on his memory and his heart.

Her coat was like a sunburst, the color ranging

from pale golden to a dark, rich brown. She was a large, powerful animal, and it was very, very easy to understand how she might have killed two men in that state. Especially after seeing her fight. She might not have experience or skill on her side, but she did have raw power, and what's more, a willingness to use it. Joined with swift reflexes and a wolf's instinct, she made a formidable opponent.

But without any experience, skill, or training, she couldn't have a real sense of her own power. She couldn't trust herself. He hoped after this, she would be comfortable enough in her new skin to request his aid.

His eyes fell shut, but his fingers continued to caress her coat. Finally, his hand stilled, resting on her gently, unmoving for the rest of the night.

12

THE LAST THING SERA EXPECTED WHEN SHE OPENED her eyes was to be alone in a dark room. She fumbled around, trying to get her bearings and find a light, and triggered some sort of alarm. A loud bell chimed again and again. Before she could find a way to silence the alarm, the door opened and a small woman in pink and yellow nursing scrubs bustled in and flipped on the lights.

"Oh, it's good to see you're awake," the woman greeted her. "How are you feeling?"

"Where am I?" Sera rasped.

"St. Catherine's. I'm Rita, your nurse this afternoon."

"The hospital?" She gasped, her hands immediately going to her stomach. "My baby. What happened to the baby?"

"The baby is fine," Rita assured her. "He's sleeping in the nursery right now and he can't wait to meet his mama."

"He's really okay?"

"Yes. He's a little small but he's a fighter. He didn't even need to be put in the incubator."

"Where's my fiancée?"

A frown marred Rita's sunny countenance for the first time. "I am sorry to tell you this. He is in the county holding facility."

"Jail?" Sera moved too quickly in her haste to jump from the bed and fly immediately to the sheriff's department to post his bail, or break him out, or cry and plead until they finally were moved to free the father of her new baby. She wasn't sure what the plan was, but the sudden pain in her lower abdomen and back halted her progress.

Rita was at her side immediately, easing her back against the bed with a gentle hand and a reassuring smile. "It's okay. He can't hurt you here."

"*Hurt* me?" Sera was too perplexed by the statement to even be angry on behalf of Seth. "He would never hurt me. What are you talking about? What happened?"

"He went wild during the delivery. He tried to attack the nurses and the doctor. And then he attacked you. That's why I always say you can't trust wolves. Why we allow them to live in our communities, I'll never know." Her eyes widened and she quickly added, "No offense meant, of course."

"Offense? I don't know what you're talking about. I just want Seth and my baby." Tears of confusion and frustration sprang to her eyes. "Please."

"Shhh, shhh, shhh. Don't cry." Rita checked the monitors and made a few rapid notes on the computer stationed by the bed. "Look, it's time for your pain management."

"I don't want to manage my pain," Sera protested. "I need to see my son. I need to find Seth."

Rita ignored her protests, plugging something into the IV attached to Sera's arm. Within seconds, warmth flooded her veins, sinking through her, enveloping her until she couldn't do anything but give into it.

When she woke again hours later, she wasn't alone. Stephanie sat next to the bed, her back straight, her eyes closed, a cell phone resting between her limp fingers. Sera turned her head to the left and saw that the shades had been pulled open, allowing her a view of the city lights and dark gray sky. *Just after dusk or just before dawn*, she thought. Judging by Stephanie's slumber, she'd put her money on dawn.

This time, Sera was careful not to move, afraid of sounding the alarm that would summon Rita to her room again. She was vaguely aware of the pain in her midsection, but it was a distant hum—something she would have ignored completely if Seth were there, holding her hand, waiting for her to wake up.

"Steph," she croaked out.

Stephanie jumped, reaching for her hand automatically. "Oh, honey, how are you feeling?"

"Where's Seth? Where's my baby?"

Stephanie took a deep breath. "Seth is currently being detained until Monday morning, when he has his court date. The baby is in the nursery. He's doing really great," Stephanie said with an encouraging smile. It seemed genuine despite her watery eyes. "But he has to stay there for a little while longer."

"I want to see him."

"Of course, honey." She squeezed Sera's hand. "We'll go see him."

"Now." The word was curt but her voice was pleading. She needed to see him; she needed to see with her own eyes that he was there, that he was real, and that he was safe.

"I'll call the nurse."

"Not Rita."

"No, Joe is on shift. Rita? Did you wake up earlier?"

Sera nodded. "She was in the room and she didn't give me a chance to see him before she dosed me up again."

"I'm sorry you woke up before I got here, honey. I didn't want you to wake up alone."

As always, Stephanie's direct kindness both startled and touched her. It was a trait she shared with Seth, and one that always brought Sera up short. She had finally learned what it would take to attract her parents' attention when they turned up for Aiza's funeral, but not for her wedding. And here was a woman who'd known her for less than a year, genuinely sorry she couldn't be there at the exact moment Sera opened her eyes.

"It's okay, I was just—"

"Scared? Confused?" Stephanie offered a wry smile. "The night didn't exactly go as planned, did it?"

"No, but as long as Seth and the baby are safe, I

won't complain. But this isn't how I wanted to spend our first night as a family. Will I be able to talk to Seth?"

"He called while you were asleep. He's fine. He's safe. He'll call again as soon as he can. I promised him that I would be at your side when he did."

"Thank you." Sera brought their clasped hands up, placing a kiss on the back of Stephanie's hand. She felt a twinge in her arm at the gesture and she noticed the tight bandage for the first time. "What is that?"

"That is where Seth bit you. That's why he's sitting in a holding cell instead of here with you."

Sera blinked. "I don't understand. I don't...is it the painkillers? Is that why I don't understand?"

"Honey, you were dying. He panicked, I guess. He fought his way in here and he bit you."

"Bit me? Why?"

"Our saliva contains the virus that causes lycanthropy. Its effect is almost immediate and it replicates quickly. One of the side effects is rapid division of cells. Your body is literally remaking itself, cell by cell, repairing damage in the process." She nodded at the bandage. "Go ahead and remove it."

Sera frowned. "Shouldn't the doctor do that?"

"Take it off. You'll see."

Sera obeyed, peeling the adhesive off and lifting the gauze to reveal perfectly skilled skin, without a visible scar. "If I'm perfectly healed, what did she...what did she give me?"

"Who?"

"The nurse. Rita."

Joe knocked and opened the door, halting Stephanie's reply, and Sera immediately gestured at the computer. "What did she give me? I want to know what was in that IV? She said it was for pain."

Joe frowned and checked his iPad. "You don't have anything ordered for pain. Why? Do you need something?"

"That nurse. Rita. She gave me something. It's got to be in there. I saw her at the computer."

Joe consulted his iPad again and shook his head. "We don't have a Rita working on this floor and there hasn't been an order placed for any narcotics. It's typically not needed in cases like yours."

"Then who...?" Sera's eyes widened. "Stephanie? Have you seen the baby?"

"I came here first. I just got here a few minutes before you woke up."

"Go. Please. Stephanie, you need to make sure he's safe. I know I sound crazy—"

"You don't sound crazy," Stephanie said, leaving

the room at a sprint. Sera's stomach dropped and she knew the truth before she heard the security code over the PA system.

The baby was gone.

13

Aiza opened her eyes to the bright morning light feeling more rested and secure than she'd felt in years. She yawned and kicked the blanket away, the sunshine warming her naked skin and fueling the sense of energy and optimism already flooding her veins. She absently took note of her surroundings, not particularly alarmed to find herself in Noah's apartment, though she had no memory of why she was there.

She was, however, surprised to discover that the man himself was asleep beside her in the bed. Not just next to her, but curled around her, his arm over her stomach, his head resting on her shoulder. She yelped and reached for the sheet, pulling it back over her chest. His slumber wasn't disturbed by her sudden noise, and she had a moment to take stock of the situation.

Had they done more than just sleep in that bed? She doubted it. Despite her nudity, he was fully dressed. Closing her eyes, she worked her way back to the first thing she could remember, which was volunteering to help Stephanie track down the Brotherhood wolves. She assumed everything went as planned, and that Noah then brought her here and fell asleep.

Aiza relaxed against the pillow and looked down at Noah's softened features. Strange, now that she was over her confusion, it felt perfectly natural to see him sleeping next to her. She reached out, tentatively brushing his hair away from his temple, letting her fingers move through the strands. Most of the time, she didn't even remember the age difference between them, but seeing him sleeping so tenderly reminded her that there must have been at least a decade separating them.

The second she pulled away, his eyes opened and his face creased into a completely unfettered smile. It was so sincere and spontaneous that Aiza caught her breath, overwhelmed to be on the receiving end of what appeared to be pure joy. Even his eyes wrinkled, and if she had any notion of leaving that bed, it completely fled her mind.

"Good morning."

"Um." Her tongue was frozen and it took a few beats before she could say, "Good morning."

"How did you sleep? Do you feel okay?" His voice was still gruff with sleep, and the smile hadn't left his eyes.

"Great and great." Now would be the perfect time to pull her arm away and try to stand up, she thought, but if she moved, she would lose the wonderful heat of his body. "I don't remember anything that happened last night, though."

"You helped Stephanie take down some bad wolves, and then I took them into custody. I brought you back here to rest." He pushed himself up, propping his head on his hand and studying her. "Seemed like you wanted to be a wolf for a while."

"I...yeah, I guess so. I hope I didn't go too far."

"No, not at all. You were perfect."

She felt herself blushing at the direct praise, so simply stated, but like his smile, too sincere to discount. Their faces were so close, and it made her blush harder to think that he was noticing her pleasure at his words. He leaned forward slightly, and she felt his breath fan over her skin. His gaze dropped to her mouth and she unconsciously parted her lips, but she didn't put any space between them. In fact, instead of leaning away, she felt herself drawn closer, as though the inches separating them were too many instead of too few.

A voice inside warned her to stay out of his reach and begged her to pull away, but it was Dwight's voice. A voice she was learning to ignore. The first touch of his lips to hers were as shocking as a bucket of ice water on a hot, summer day. She froze, and he pulled back immediately, his brow furrowed into a question.

"I'm sorry. I thought..." He shook his head and pushed the sheet away, swinging his legs over the side of the bed, sitting on the edge with his back to her. "That was not appropriate. I apologize."

"Wait." She placed her hand on his arm, a thrill running through her at the way his hard muscles felt beneath his smooth skin. "I didn't mean...you didn't do anything wrong."

"Actually, I did."

"Is there a rule against kissing your star witness?"

He threw a wry smile over his shoulder. "Yes, there is."

"Oh. Is it a very big rule?"

"There are no such things as little rules when it comes to working for the government."

"I see. So, is another kiss too big of a risk?"

"Well, that depends."

"On what?"

He looked over his shoulder again. "On who kisses who. I mean, I probably shouldn't kiss you. But if you kiss me, technically you didn't break any rules."

"I do love a good technicality," she murmured as she rose to her knees, holding the sheet to her chest. She leaned against his back, tilting her head so that her long hair flowed around them, creating a curtain as she sought his mouth with hers.

Now that she had a chance to process how good his lips felt, how good his skin smelled, and how much she wanted to touch him, she could kiss him with a bit more aplomb. It began as a closed-lip inquiry; she was the first one to change, parting her lips in a subtle invitation. An invitation he seemed all too happy to accept. His tongue slid over her bottom lip before probing further, brushing into her mouth. She leaned back against the pillow, opening further to his kiss, pulling him with her.

At that point in Aiza's life, long, slow kisses were nothing but distant memories. She kept expecting him to grow bored and press for more, but one hand lingered on her shoulder, the other cupping the side of her face. She wasn't in any rush to change. His mouth felt amazing against hers, and it was clear that not only did the man enjoy kissing, he was very good at it. Dominant without being demanding, sensual, passionate and yet calmly deliberate.

Heat flooded her, tightening her inner muscles, making her flesh throb. A surprising ache flared deep inside her core, and that only fanned the flames. She slid her fingers through his hair and over his shoulders, sighing in frustration at the feel of cotton instead of skin. She felt his lips curl upward slightly, and then he pulled back and yanked the T-shirt over his head, allowing her access to the texture and warmth of his skin.

The first thing she found was a scar. Then there was another. And another. It didn't take long to realize that his body was a topographical map of bad memories. Throughout her explorations, their kisses remained slow and steady, but her hips were starting to move, her body seeking more. He gripped her hips, pulling her against him, and she gasped as his erection pushed against her thigh, straining against the material of his boxers.

She reached for his length without hesitation,

earning a sigh from him as she pulled him free of the shorts. Once she had him in hand, she wasn't quite sure what to do. She didn't want the kisses to end, but her flesh was throbbing in time with his, and he was already so close. All she would have to do is guide him to the juncture of her thighs, let the tip drag over her swollen clit and then deep inside.

The thought was enough to make her hips shift, her breath coming quicker and quicker. He broke away from her mouth, his lips swollen, his eyes heavy-lidded. She stared back, her tongue suddenly feeling too big for her mouth, blocking whatever words she might think to utter.

"I have a condom," he said thickly.

Now was the time to pull herself together, to gather her wits and tell him they should stop. But it was so hard to think of a single reason not to take everything he had to offer. She nodded, her pulse hammering at the base of her throat. He rolled away from her and losing the heat of his body was almost the cold slap to the face she needed to wake up from her hormone-drenched daze. She shivered, her nipples becoming taut as the chill chased through her. Absently, she ran her fingertips over her nipples and shivered again, this time with anticipation. He must have caught her movement from the corner of his eye, because he was back on her in a flash, his fingers closing around her wrists, his lips covering her nipple.

Aiza gasped and arched her back, eyes rolling backwards as his teeth teased the sensitive flesh. Her nipples were already hard as rocks, but somehow her skin grew tighter, the sensation almost unbearable, and yet so sweet that she couldn't even try to pull away from him. He shifted his attention to her other nipple, his hands disappearing while his tongue swirled around the pebbled flesh in slow circles. Her hips began to move in time with his languid caresses, her clit throbbing with each sweep of his tongue.

Her hands moved over his shoulders and down his back, finding new scars, sliding over bunched muscles and smooth skin. She felt magnetized everywhere their bodies touched, completely unable to pull away from him or allow even a centimeter of space between them. Her mouth watered for him, her lips tingling for more kisses, her tongue yearning for the taste of salt on his skin.

His hands returned to her body, palms gliding over her hips and up her ribs to cup her breasts. He left a hot trail of kisses over her chest and up her neck, pausing to suck on the sensitive skin below her jaw until she yelped and bucked her hips, bringing her back into direct contact with his erection. It felt like being touched with a live-wire, and the fine hair on her arms and the back of her neck stood on end. Her thighs were slick with excitement, and she realized it'd had been a *very* long time since she felt so ready for a man.

"Noah...Noah...God honey, I'm ready."

He moaned and reached between them, gripping his length and sliding the tip over her lips. She caught her breath, her flesh already so sensitive that just a whisper of contact was almost too much to stand. She lifted her hips, hooking her legs around his hips, and guided him forward as the tip of his engorged dick easily entered her.

He met no resistance as he sheathed himself, and Aiza had to press her lips together to keep from shouting. He fit perfectly inside of her and her mouth instantly ran dry, her body clenching down around his shaft. He moaned, his forehead touching hers, his mouth just an inch away from hers. The sound came from deep in his throat and it almost sounded like a growl. Like a wolf calling for his mate.

Aiza already felt like she was on the edge of some madness, but that low sound woke something

primal inside of her. She clawed at his back, not realizing her nails had started to grow, and suddenly, she
was reminded of her enhanced sense of smell. The
scent of his body fed her hunger, and the scent of
their coupling was like a fog settling over her mind.

He rotated his hips in a slow, maddening, perfect
circle after each snapping thrust. She moaned,
nipping at his lips, biting at his throat and neck,
shaking every time he made a sound of pleasure; of
encouragement. He made her heady, like she was
drunk on a fine wine, her senses both sharpened
and dulled, her body uncoordinated, powerless, and
yet, she moved with him in perfect tandem. Maybe
she was following, maybe she was leading, but she
couldn't be sure where her body ended and the lines
of his began.

He stopped without warning and she barely had
the chance to see the look of concentration on his
face before he flipped her over onto her knees. She
barely had a chance to brace herself before he was
plunging inside of her again. This time she couldn't
stop her shout of pleasure, the sound tearing from
her throat and echoing in her ears. The friction was
too much against her aching flesh, and the new
angle brought the head of his cock directly against
her G-spot with each sharp thrust. She dropped her

head, her long hair shielding her face but doing nothing to muffle her cries of ecstasy. She was too far gone to care if the whole world heard her, though.

She could feel her orgasm building and sense the imminence of her breaking point. She used to go sledding every winter, and she felt that same sense of recklessness, of careening out of control and abandoning herself to the forces hurling through her body through space.

Noah buried his hand in her hair, holding her close to the scalp, pulling her back against his chest and seeking out her mouth. His lips had been so sweet before, but now they were hard and demanding, as though he meant to mark her with the heat of his mouth. The demanding pressure of his lips and the flick of his tongue against hers completely undid her. He flexed his fingers, sending a cascade of chills from her scalp down her spine and thrust forward with each force to make her see stars.

The world spun out around her, her entire body throbbing, the pulse of her heart matching the relentless rhythm of his body. Her pussy locked down around him, twitching and flexing until she felt him falter and thrust forward with a final moan of completion. They collapsed to the mattress together, and it was so easy to fold against his body, to rest in his arms and try to catch her breath.

"Aiza, I—"

She never learned what he wanted to say. The sudden ringing of his phone pulled his attention from her and the moment between them was completely shattered. "I have to answer that."

She took advantage of distraction to flee the bed for the bathroom, suddenly in need of space and a splash of cold water to the face. Aiza didn't quite recognize the woman in the mirror with tousled hair and the look of glutted satisfaction in her eyes.

It wasn't just the heat of the moment. She wanted to sleep with him again. She wanted to *be* with him again. More than she'd wanted anything else in a long, long time.

Unfortunately, she didn't know what to do with this knowledge. He clearly wanted her, too, but that didn't mean they should make this a regular thing— especially given the extenuating circumstances. Now was hardly the time to start a relationship, and she had little interest in a one-night stand.

A soft knock on her door pulled her from her thoughts. "Aiza?"

She opened the door. "Is everything okay?"

He shook his head, his mouth set in a frown. She

didn't know what she expected, but it definitely wasn't this. "The baby has been...kidnapped."

"Kidnapped? From the hospital? Somebody took the baby from the hospital?"

"Yes."

"It was the Brotherhood, wasn't it?"

"There are no leads yet."

"No leads?" Aiza stared at him, waiting for him to answer, to say anything that made sense. "What are you talking about?"

"Aiza, there's no evidence."

"We know exactly who did it!"

"I know that. You know that. But as of yet, there's no evidence. As soon as I have a piece of evidence, we can take it before a judge and—"

"Isn't Seth sitting in a jail cell right now because there's no judge around to set bail? How long are you going to have to wait—how long is my *nephew* going to have to wait before you do something?"

"I've got to go."

"I'm coming with you."

"No you're not."

"Yes, I am."

"Aiza, please, I don't need this right now."

"You don't need *what* right now?" She folded her arms. "Am I under arrest?"

"Is that what it will take to keep you here?"

"Yes."

"Then yes. I'm placing you under arrest, Aiza Simpson."

"What's the charge?"

"Seriously, Aiza? I just…" He took a deep breath. "Aiza, my alpha is under arrest and in extreme distress and I can't do anything about it. His son is missing and until I can find one single scrap of evidence, my hands are tied. I don't know what I would do if you were hurt, too. I need you to be safe."

"Because I'm a witness?"

"No. Because—" Noah's phone erupted again and he growled with frustration, bringing it to his ear. "Yes? I'll be there in—I'll be there." She knew from the tone of his voice that he was speaking with Stephanie. "I've got to go. Please, stay here. I'll call you." She didn't want to delay him for another moment, so she only nodded.

14

"I'm not staying here," Sera stated flatly. The hospital room was driving her insane by inches, and she itched to flee the restrictive walls, but Stephanie deemed the cabin too unsafe after the earlier ambush. "I'm not going to sit here and do nothing while those *motherfuckers* have my baby."

Stephanie's eyebrow went up, but she didn't offer an argument. "I can't make you stay here."

"I'm going to get him back." She lifted her chin, still expecting a challenge, not knowing what she would do if Stephanie pushed back. Did Stephanie have any actual authority over her now? Would Stephanie resort to violence to stop her? Sera didn't feel weak, but she had no idea of her true strength, nor did she know anything about fighting. Or being a wolf. "And I need your help, Stephanie. Please."

"Of course," she said, without a moment of hesitation.

Sera's eyes widened. Somehow, she hadn't expected that. "Really?"

"Those motherfuckers took my whole family. I'm not going to let them do it again. If Seth were here, he'd say the same thing."

"Well...I don't know what to do."

Stephanie's smile was grim and more than a little scary. "I've spent the past ten years building a spy network throughout the Pacific Northwest. I'll get a location."

"That's how you were able to find Aiza?"

Stephanie nodded. "They don't do much without me knowing about it." She frowned and shook her head. "But I still didn't see this coming."

"Well, how could you have? How could they have, for that matter?"

"There was an ambush on the compound. The two events might have been related, or maybe whoever took the baby heard about Seth's arrest. They do monitor the police scanner."

"So they heard Seth was arrested and somehow

hatched a kidnapping plan on the fly? Why? There has to be a reason, Stephanie."

"They're assholes."

Sera's head snapped up at the strange yet beautifully familiar voice. "Aiza."

Stephanie moved immediately, placing herself between Sera and her sister, shoulders square. Hurt flashed over Aiza's face at the aggressive gesture, and Sera's heart jumped to her throat.

"Look, I'm not here to start a fight." Aiza held up both hands and looked from Stephanie to Sera, her eyes pleading. "I'm here to help."

"How did you know?" Sera asked.

They called Noah. He wanted me to stay put and maybe I shouldn't be here, but I knew you weren't going to wait around for some judge to issue a warrant." She tilted her head. "I was right, wasn't I?"

"You're right." She blinked rapidly, trying to bring her rapidly rising emotions under control. There was so much she wanted to ask, so much she wanted to say, but all of that had to wait. "And thank you. Your help is very much appreciated. I just don't exactly know what we'll need your help with quite yet."

Stephanie's phone started to ring, and she paused to check the screen before answering. When she saw the number, she quickly brought the phone to her ear. "Seth? Are you alright? Yes, of course. She's right here."

Sera accepted the phone with trembling fingers and her tears threatened to spill again as she heard Seth's voice. "Sera, honey?"

"They took him."

"I know. Noah's here. He told me. They're working on finding him right now. They've got local and federal officials combing the area. There's an Amber Alert out. They're going to find him."

"You don't know that."

"Sera—"

"You don't know that," Sera said with a brittle edge. "I'm going to find him."

"Sera, honey, no."

"No? Just because you can't do anything doesn't mean I'm going to just sit here and twiddle my thumbs."

The silence felt heavy between them. Finally, Seth said, "They're dangerous. What if they find our son just in time for him to lose his mother?"

"*Who* are they, Seth? Who are they to do this to us? To you? To Aiza?"

"They're a gang of low-lives, thieves and leeches. They don't make anything, they only subsist on what they can take. They're not smart, but they're strong and they're mean, and there's enough of them to get what they want, most of the time."

"What do they want from *you*?" Sera just wanted to understand. "Is it land? Money? Do they just like to see you hurt?"

"I'd wager it's all three. They'd get our territory and everything we leave behind."

"Somebody has to stop them."

"That's what Noah and a lot of other good men and women are working on right now. You don't need to put yourself in harm's way."

"I love you."

"Sera—"

"I'll see you soon."

"Sera, listen—" Even though it sent a shard of pain through her chest, she ended the call and handed the phone back to Stephanie. "Is there some place safe we can go and make a plan?"

"I've got a place." Her attention jumped over to Aiza. "Somewhere Noah won't come looking."

"Let's go." Sera had never felt so resolute, so confident, in her life. But she'd never felt this sort of power thrumming through her veins.

And she'd never had a better reason to fight.

15

ADAM BLINKED INTO THE DARKNESS, TRYING TO MAKE out any shadow or clue of where he was and how he ended up there. The last thing he remembered was stepping outside of the bar. It had been a little after midnight, and the lot was still full, the sound of music and drinking drifting from the door behind him. He hadn't heard anything else. He didn't have any memory of seeing anybody or even of the blow that knocked him out. The lump to the side of his temple was as big as a goose egg and throbbing like hell.

The floor beneath him was carpeted, and there might have been a window to his right, but it looked like it was covered in blackout paper. There was no light from the outside and no way to tell what time it was. He closed his eyes and extended his senses, bringing the wolf to the surface. He caught the scent of another wolf, and his lip automatically curled, exposing his sharp canines.

He recognized her scent easily. It still lingered in the bar, and most annoyingly, in his office. When he'd learned that Aiza was still alive, he'd been annoyed at Dwight's incompetence, but he thought the situation had been handled. Isn't that exactly what he sent Braxton to do? He resolved to kill that pup at the first opportunity—that level of incompetence couldn't be allowed to exist within the Brotherhood.

Adam summoned the rest of his power, prepared to shift into his wolf form and find the woman responsible for his inconvenience, but he found he was unable to change. When he tried again, the shackle on his wrist began to burn.

"Silver chains. That goddamned bitch."

So shifting was out of the question. With nothing else to occupy him, he leaned back against the wall and imagined what he would do to Aiza once he was done skinning Braxton's pelt. It was a shame things worked out the way they did because he always thought she looked pretty good for someone her age. Dwight had been an incompetent idiot most of his life, but he did know how to pick them. Most wolves fought for their territory and wealth, but that had never been Dwight's style. Unfortunately, Dwight's style tended to leave messes behind and Adam always found himself embroiled with the cleanup.

"Ai-*za*! I know you're here, honey." He paused, waiting for any response. "Is this about your shitty bar? I did you a favor by taking over that rat hole. It's hemorrhaging money!"

No response. He wasn't especially surprised. She clearly had a plan if she had the foresight to obtain and use silver chains. He gave the chains a good rattle before shouting Aiza's name again. "Look, I'm awake! Let's talk."

"What do you want to talk about?"

The hair on the back of Adam's neck stood on end. That was *not* Aiza's voice. His nostrils flared and he realized that he'd missed something before. Or maybe he hadn't missed it. Maybe they'd masked her scent somehow. But there was no mistaking the fact that he was speaking to a Longtail.

"Where am I?"

"Someplace safe."

"What do you want?"

"Just want some information, Adam. I don't want

to hurt you. Unless you need help remembering the details. Or if I don't like what I hear."

"Information about what?" Adam asked, his tone neutral.

Braxton had got a message out from the detention center—at least the pup was smart enough not to call him directly—indicating there had been a bloody skirmish with the Longtail pack. Did they know it was on his orders? They must have. Why else would he be there? But which one of those idiots had talked? And what had they said?

"Where's the baby?"

"The what?"

Pain erupted in his head as the words left his mouth, and he realized somebody was standing behind him. Somebody who had absolutely no qualms about knocking his head in. He blinked, trying to get his eyes to focus in the dark.

"Try again."

"I don't know what you're talking about."

Another blow, this one hard enough to make his teeth sink into his tongue. He spat the blood out and tried to peer around to his left, but the room was too dark and he couldn't make out anything more than a vague shape.

"Give me his phone." A moment later, the screen

illuminated enough of his captor's face for him to recognize the resemblance. Definitely a Longtail. "See, I don't believe you because you got this message. 'Package picked up. Delivered to safe local. Will wait.' So, where's the package?"

"That's just booze."

"So the package is at the bar?"

It might have been the rapid blows to the head—another one followed close behind the question—that led him to give an honest answer. Or maybe he was just confused by his own lie. But he blurted out, "Yes, yes it's there. Please, stop."

But his captor didn't stop and his jaw cracked from the force of her fist smashing into the side of his face. The world turned into a murky ocean, swimming around him in thick waves. He made out one voice saying, "I think we should go to the bar."

"I don't like the thought of leaving him alone here."

"He won't be alone for long. The cleaning crew will be here to take care of him."

Another hard blow and the world turned red and then black.

16

CYN DIDN'T KNOW ANYTHING ABOUT TAKING CARE OF babies. She was definitely the least qualified person she knew to be responsible for any child, but especially one as small and delicate as the boy in her arms. Apparently, she was supposed to know what to do just because she was a female, like it was just built-in knowledge. Like she could just pick up a newborn baby and know why it was crying, what it needed, and how to provide it.

"Shut that goddamned kid up!" One of the bikers bellowed. She couldn't keep track of their names and had long ago given up on ever remembering who was who. It didn't really matter anyway. All they ever did was yell, throw things at her and yell at her some more. She really didn't need to know their names. Now they were yelling at her because the goddamned *newborn baby* wouldn't stop crying.

"Please stop crying, baby. Please stop. Come on." She held him and rocked him, but that did nothing to stop the noise. He probably needed food, but she sure wasn't going to produce anything for him. Could babies drink cow milk? It was milk, after all. Did it need to be warmed up? It seemed like she shouldn't be feeding the baby cold cow milk, but wasn't something better than nothing? Especially if it would buy a few minutes of peace and quiet?

There was no milk in the bar. All they had was heavy cream. That seemed like an even worse idea than regular milk, but she had to do *something*.

"If that little bastard doesn't shut up, I'm gonna—"

"You shut up, Merv. You're worse than the baby."

"Go fuck yourself."

"Both of you shut the fuck up. Where's Adam? He should be back by now."

"How the fuck should I know? It's not like he checks in with me."

It occurred to Cyn that she should simply slip out the back and flee with the baby, but these were wolves. Ruthless wolves who cared nothing about Cyn's life and even less about the baby. They would use their powerful sense of smell to track her down and kill them both. Cyn was not ready to die. She was ready to get the fuck out of that bar and never serve drinks or see a baby again, but she was not ready to die.

She took the baby to the back of the bar, in the little nook that served as their kitchen when they used to serve food. When they used to have customers. Now there wasn't a single paying regular —just all these Brotherhood goons with their bad manners and ill-tempered profanities. Since they didn't pay, they didn't tip, but that didn't stop them from ordering her around all night. Soon after Aiza disappeared, she tried to leave. She tried to leave again when Aiza reappeared. Both times, Adam had shown up at her house and insisted for her to return to work.

He had a most persuasive argument: a Saturday night special with the tip sawed off. So Cyn had returned to work, and every few weeks, he'd hand her a few bills in a wrinkled envelope and she accepted it with a smile that said *well, at least I'm not dead yet.*

The sudden appearance of a random baby put a small crinkle in her plan of not dying. Not only did the baby distract her from fetching their beer, peanuts and pretzels, but she couldn't get it to stop its endless crying. What if they did decide to hurt the kid?

Cyn shuddered, horrified by the line of thought she was actually following. The one they'd forced her to embark on.

She mixed the cream she found with water and warmed it over the stove top, while she cradled the baby in one arm and made cooing sounds. Her cooing didn't help, and probably only exacerbated the situation. She wished she could cry right along with the kid, but she didn't dare make a noise they might overhear.

She hadn't asked where the kid came from and she was pretty sure she didn't want to know. It was clear, though, that however they'd obtained the child, it wasn't via a careful plan with that outcome as the articulated goal. Even Adam seemed nonplussed. Cyn wished she could grab him and shake him and shout, *what the fuck are you doing? This kid has parents! There will be cops!* But she didn't dare even say peep in his direction. All she could do was keep her head down and hope she didn't get caught in the inevitable crossfire.

When the top of the watery cream broke with a bubble, she removed it from the heat and stared at it doubtfully. She didn't have a bottle—unless she could use a beer bottle or a tequila bottle once she drained it of its contents, but she didn't think either would work. The baby needed a nipple and there definitely wasn't a working one of those in the bar.

"Fuck, kid. What am I supposed to do?"

The baby squalled in response, its tiny hands squeezed into useless fists. He would probably be cute, if he ever stopped screaming like a scalded cat. Her eyes darted around the room until she saw the pile of clean rags on the counter. Once upon a time, they would have been folded and put away, but now there was no time for such niceties. It was a miracle she'd had time to wash the rags at all. She grabbed one and dipped a corner in the cooling liquid, then held the rag over the baby's lips. Drops of the cream fell on the baby's lips and far from soothing him, it only made him howl with new ferocity.

"Goddamnit! What the hell are you doing back there? I said to shut the kid up!"

"I'm trying the best I can," Cyn shouted back,

unmindful of the potential consequences for taking that particular tone.

"What did you just say to me?" The words grew louder with each syllable, and though she couldn't see his approach, she knew he was getting closer. She shrank back, clutching the baby close to her chest, her heart in her throat.

The one she thought of as *Bruiser* appeared. He was easily six and a half feet tall and it seemed like he was at least that wide and half that thick. His head was mostly bald except for the ring of bright red curls circling his dome just above the ears and the ZZ-Top-length red beard. That beard was the most disgusting thing Cyn had ever seen. It was always wet from beer and full of crumbs and ashes and God knew what else. Now it was only inches from her face as he loomed over her, his face set in a stony glare.

"I'm doing the best I can," Cyn repeated, much lower, unable to make eye contact. That didn't stop him from taking another half step closer. He stood so close she couldn't take a breath without getting a mouthful of his foul odor, so rank it made her eyes water.

"Well, Adam left me in charge. Give me that baby."

She reflexively clutched the child closer. "I'm...I'm trying to...trying to feed him. If you'll just give me some room." Each word was a struggle, since her entire body was paralyzed with fear and her mouth didn't want to cooperate and her lips were numb.

"I said hand it over." He reached for the baby with one hand and used the other to grab her face. She tried to twist away from his grip, but his massive fingers held her in place, distracting her while he easily plucked the child from her arms. He shoved her to the ground and stepped back, his yellow teeth gleaming in his rotten smile. "Now we'll get some peace and quiet around here."

Cyn didn't see where the wolf came from. It was nothing but a blur of white fur and a growl so low Cyn felt it rather than heard it. Bruiser roared and then went silent as he hit the ground, blood coming from the back of his broken neck. Cyn opened her mouth, but the scream was muffled by a sudden hand over her mouth. She stiffened, her heart jumping to her throat with a new rush of fear.

"Shh. It's okay."

Aiza. The tension drained from her. For the first time in months, the ache in her stomach eased and the tears gathering in her eyes were from relief.

Another woman arrived and scooped the baby out of the dead man's arms, cradling it to her chest with such tenderness that Cyn knew she must be the mother.

"How many are in the front?" Aiza asked.

"Five, I think. They were playing cards."

"There are only *five* people out there?"

"The bar is closed. Now it's just Adam's clubhouse."

Aiza's mouth set in a firm line and the look in her eye told Cyn it was time to clean house. "Get out of here. Go home, lock the door, and get some sleep. Take a couple days off."

"They're dangerous. You should call the cops."

"The cops are on their way. Everything's going to be fine as soon as I take care of these assholes."

"We should get out of here, too," the woman with the baby said.

"Go on ahead. Stephanie can take you back to the hospital. I'm getting these assholes out of my place."

The wolf who took out Bruiser had turned into a statuesque, leggy blonde. A *naked,* leggy blonde. The sort of leggy blonde that Cyn very much liked to see naked, and she felt her face turn a vibrant shade of red as her gaze lingered on the woman.

"You can't take on all of them by yourself," Stephanie said.

"I'm not leaving my bar."

"Then I'll stay and help."

"You should take Sera and the baby back to the hospital. I've got this under control."

Cyn could see that her boss had no intention of leaving until all the bikers were dead or gone. "I can drive them to the hospital."

Some silent communication passed before the three of them before Aiza nodded. "Thank you, Cyn."

Cyn stole one more glance of Stephanie before nodding and hurried with Sera out the back exit to her car. Once they were on the road with the bar in the rearview mirror, Cyn ventured with a tentative, "So, it's good to see you again." The woman had come to the bar more than once after Aiza's supposed death, searching for more information. "That's your baby?"

"It is."

"I, uh, did my best to help him. But I think he's hungry."

"Thank you. It's good to see you, too."

"So... Aiza's not dead."

"It's a long story," Sera said as she placed the

baby at her breast. "And I don't even know most of it. But..." She gazed down at her son, and even in the dark, Cyn could see her soft smile. "But it feels like a miracle."

Cyn, who had experienced her own miracle that night, could only nod.

17

THERE WERE SEVEN WOLVES IN THE FRONT OF THE BAR, not five, but they were all pretty hammered on the free beer and spirits Adam allowed them. Caught up in their poker game and not registering anything except relief from the sudden silence, they didn't notice Aiza slinking from the back of the bar or Stephanie coming around from the other side. The two struck in unison, instantly taking out two of the gang members with bites behind their necks.

Of the five remaining, three immediately transformed into wolves and two jumped away from the table, eyes wide. Aiza and Stephanie attacked as one, already moving together as though they'd been watching each other's backs for a lifetime. Stephanie had the skill that Aiza lacked, but her pure vicious strength made up for her lack of practiced reflexes.

And she was more than vicious—she was furious. She was *beyond* furious. And she wasn't just fighting for her life; she was fighting for her territory and she was either going to win or she was going to die trying. There were no other options, and Aiza understood that to the very core of her being. And it was that knowledge that fueled each snap of her jaws, each growl and bodily attack.

Still, no matter how hard she fought, she couldn't bring them down. Soon, she was on the defensive, trying to protect herself from a series of swift attacks. There were three, maybe four on her, and she had no sense of where Stephanie was, if she was hurt or if she fought on. There was a pain in her hind quarter and in her side and the scent of blood was stronger than ever, filling her nostrils and driving her into a frenzy.

Aiza howled as her back leg went out from under her. That was the opening the wolves were looking for, and once Aiza lost ground, she couldn't regain it. She tried to get away from them, but they had her backed against the bar. She howled again, calling for Stephanie, but there was no response. There was too much blood, too much chaos, to sense her, and the edges around Aiza's vision started to turn black.

Some part of her knew the fight was over, but she wasn't going to stop until she literally couldn't move.

A sudden gunshot startled all the wolves, stopping the vicious fight for the space of a heartbeat. Aiza took advantage of the opening to put some space between her and her foes, and when the fighting resumed, the number of participants had doubled. The new arrivals drove the Brotherhood wolves back, away from Aiza's wounded frame and Stephanie's bleeding body. Aiza sank to the floor, whimpering and dazed, the ground tilting and rocking beneath her.

"Aiza! Stephanie!"

Noah's voice pulled her attention up, but she still couldn't move so she barked to get his attention. He raced to her side and ran his hands along her sides and back, searching for injuries.

"It's okay, sweetheart. Everything's going to be okay. We're going to get you to a doctor. Wait for me here."

She put her muzzle down in her paws and released her breath with a long sigh. Federal agents and emergency response personnel swarmed the bar, capturing the Brotherhood wolves and dragging them away. Aiza remained still amongst the chaos, growling at anyone who ventured too close, until Noah returned and carried her away from the chaos.

18

"Knock knock." Aiza stuck her head past the office door. "Mind if I come in?"

"Come in, come in," Stephanie said, ushering her inside the appropriated office while Sera placed a sleeping baby in the pack-and-play. "How's it looking out there?"

"Everything's perfect," Aiza assured them. The bar had been transformed for Sera and Seth's ceremony, and it was full of members of the pack, friends, and even their brother Steve and his family. Aiza had taken charge of many of the details due to Stephanie's injuries and recovery time, throwing herself into the planning of the ceremony, juggling it with the responsibilities of reopening the bar. For the past three months, she woke up early, went to bed late, and made it a point to have no spare time for anything.

Stephanie glanced between the sisters and then nodded. "I'm going to go make sure Seth has his cufflinks."

"You look beautiful," Aiza said, full of sudden emotion at the sight of her younger sister, radiant and beaming with excitement.

Sera looked down at her new dress—lacy and off-white—with a shy smile. "Thank you. And thank you for everything you've done."

"It was truly my pleasure. I'm just glad that I'm here to see it."

"Me, too." Sera looked up with eyes brimming full of emotion and in that moment, she wasn't the grown woman, a wife and mother, but the little girl who used to follow Aiza around and make up silly stories. Her constant companion, whether she necessarily wanted her baby sister to shadow her or not. All the years that separated them were gone and Aiza felt a sudden surge of tears. She could hold them back, barely, but she couldn't stop herself from pulling Sera into an emotional embrace.

"I'm so sorry," Aiza said. "I'm sorry I left you and I'm sorry I disappeared. I should have stayed in touch. I should have told you..."

Sera returned her hug with an extra-long squeeze and kissed her cheek. "Honey, thank you, but I don't care about any of that. I'm so happy you're here now. I'm so happy I have my sister back."

"Not only that, but a gorgeous husband and a perfect baby."

"It's honestly more than I ever expected."

"But the very least of what you deserve."

Sera gave her another hug and then stepped back. "This place is pretty great, too."

"Thanks." Aiza looked around with a familiar swell of pride. She'd completely redone the interior of the bar, reclaiming it as something more in line with her vision for the grand reopening of Aiza's Tavern. It would still be three months before she'd be ready to reopen for business, but she was right on time and on track. Soon, she was sure, everything would be back to normal and she'd feel like herself again.

"Are there a lot of people out there?"

"We're nearly at capacity."

"Did Noah make it?"

"Oh, I didn't notice," Aiza said with feigned indifference. He was there. And she did notice his presence the second he walked through the door. His scent hit her first, and then all of her senses screamed that he was there.

After Adam's arrest and the subsequent rounding up of his cronies, the Wolf Brotherhood started to weaken. Noah had been as busy with the continuing investigation as Aiza had been with the bar and their paths rarely crossed. Aiza told herself that was for the best, but it was hard to remember that when she actually saw him. "It's time. Are you ready?"

Sera nodded and checked on baby Charlie once more, then turned up the baby monitor. "I am."

Aiza texted the DJ, and a moment later, she heard the music change, signaling everyone to take their seats. She offered Sera her arm, another wave of pride washing through her as she prepared to walk her sister down the aisle. They stepped out of the office and all of the guests rose from their seats. Aiza recognized some of them, but the only person she cared about, the only one she could see, was Noah, halfway down and sitting right on the edge of the aisle. She made it a point not to look at him at all.

Instead, she focused on Seth, who was undeniably handsome. In her effort to reconnect with her sister, she'd gotten to know him better, and they'd reached a new understanding. She didn't know if Seth would have fully forgiven her for what she'd done, but he didn't seem to hate her anymore. Stephanie had also been crucial in the forging of a relationship with him; it seemed he couldn't resist the combined efforts of his beloved and his co-alpha.

Now he stood at the end of the aisle, gaze locked on Sera, his smile full of pride, his eyes full of admiration. When it came down to it, Aiza really didn't care what Seth thought of her. She only cared about the way he looked at her sister—never with anything less than his complete and utter devotion. Sera, for her part, always had a bit of wonder in her smile, as though she couldn't quite believe that this was her life. That she wasn't dreaming.

Aiza risked a look at Noah as they passed by, her heart twisting in her chest while her stomach fluttered. He looked tired, undeniably, but he cleaned up very, very well. She couldn't tell if the woman sitting next to him was a date or one of his extended family members—they didn't share a resemblance, and their legs were touching. Why were their legs touching?

Because you had to cram in extra chairs. And it's none of your concern anyway. Their bodies could touch all night, for all you care.

Once they reached the waiting groom, Aiza gave Sera a hug and a kiss on the cheek, then passed her arm to Seth's and took her place to the side. Stephanie stood with Seth, leaning on the crutch she held in her right hand. Their eyes met and she offered a small smile before the officiant asked everyone to take their seats.

The words of the ceremony flowed over Aiza—she was sure it was all very beautiful, but she was too distracted by Noah's presence. She'd managed not to think about him for the past three months, but only by working herself down to the bone. Was he looking at her? It was impossible to tell, since the entire room was looking at the happy couple and she was standing right next to them.

She knew she would have to speak to him, sooner or later. She certainly wouldn't be able to avoid him all night. And she couldn't even say for sure why she wanted to avoid him, except for the fact that, paradoxically, she wanted nothing more than to see him, to talk to him, to touch him... To hold him.

The ceremony was surprisingly short and ended with a kiss so passionate that Aiza was sure it made most of the guests uncomfortable. When Seth lifted his head, they were both beaming and somebody whooped, prompting the whole crowd to laugh and for Seth to shout, "Let's party!"

The DJ immediately blasted music and people started folding the chairs and moving them aside, opening up the area for dancing. The baby monitor crackled with static and then Charlie started to cry, startled awake by the sudden noise. Sera's head immediately swung around, but Aiza gestured for her to stay and enjoy herself; she would take care of the baby. She was all too glad to make an escape from the party and the people she didn't know—and the one man she knew all too well.

"Come here, little guy. What's wrong," she said, as she lifted the baby from his bed. "Hmm? What's wrong? Don't like all that noise? It's just your mommy and daddy having a big ol' party. It's alright."

She never thought of herself as a "baby person," but she did like little Charlie. He had big, deep blue eyes, an amazing thatch of black hair, and he rarely cried. He was already quieting down, comforted by his aunt's low voice and soft chest.

"You're a natural with him."

Aiza spun around. "Oh. Noah. Hi."

"Hi. That was a beautiful ceremony, wasn't it?"

"Oh. Gorgeous."

"What was your favorite part?"

"Um, well, the vows were really touching. Especially when Seth said he would, you know, always cherish her."

"Yeah. But I don't think he said that."

"Oh." She offered a sheepish smile. "I wasn't listening to closely."

"Yeah. Me neither."

"Then how do you know he didn't say that?"

It was his turn to smile. "I don't. I was a little distracted."

"Distracted?"

"Yeah. I was. Um, the bar's really come along. You've done a lot of work. It's looking great."

"Thank you."

"When's the grand opening?"

"In a few months. I don't have a date yet."

"Well, let me know. I don't want to miss it."

"I'll do that."

"I...uh...Aiza. I actually wanted to talk to you—"

"Oh, there you are!" The woman he'd been sitting next to burst through the door and startled Charlie awake. He immediately started crying and she took Noah's arm. "Come on. I want to dance."

"I was just helping Aiza with the baby."

"You should go dance. I've got this under control," Aiza said quickly with a smile that probably looked as forced as it felt. "We'll, uh, catch up later."

"Okay, yeah. We'll talk later." He followed his date out the door and Aiza sank into her chair, clutching the baby even closer. They were *definitely* not going to talk later. She was going to sit in that office with Charlie for the rest of the night, until it was time to send everybody home and clean the place up. It was a bit antisocial on her part, but she didn't think anyone would notice or care. Besides, Charlie needed her more than anyone out there did, anyhow.

It wasn't long before he fell asleep again, and an exhausted Aiza found herself staring at the top of the baby's head, watching the light reflect off of his fine hair. She had no idea how long she sat there like that before a soft knock on the door alerted her to the fact that she had another visitor.

"Hey. You're missing the party," Stephanie said.

"Is everyone having a good time?"

"They're having a great time. You want to join them? I can watch him."

Aiza shook her head. "Not really."

"Are you feeling okay?"

"Yeah, I'm fine. Just...tired. Like I've run out of gas."

"Well, that makes sense. You've been working hard to pull all of this together. Everything's perfect, by the way."

"Thank you."

Stephanie nodded. "Well, if you just need to rest, I'll leave you alone. I thought maybe you were back here hiding from Noah."

Aiza blanched. "I don't know why you would think that."

She shrugged. "Just a hunch. Look, there's a real cute girl out there and she's been making eyes at me all night, so I'm going to ask her to dance. Maybe you should consider it, too."

"Consider dancing with Cyn?"

"No, consider dancing with the very cute guy who has been waiting on you all night."

"Isn't Noah your cousin? Are you allowed to think he's cute?"

"I am when it's an objective fact. He's miserable out there right now and it's bringing down the whole party."

Aiza frowned. "Why is he miserable?"

"Because he thinks you hate him. Or you're mad

at him. Or he's fucked everything up with you. Has he?"

"He hasn't...look, he hasn't fucked anything up because there's nothing to fuck up. He was just doing his job and now that job is over."

"Really?" She sat on the corner of the desk. "You think you were just a job to him?"

"Yeah. Of course."

"And he was just your bodyguard? He meant nothing more to you?"

Aiza sighed. "It doesn't matter, okay? This past year has been so fucked up and I just don't think...how can I...he deserves better than to be caught up in the mess of my life."

"If you're not ready to be in a relationship right now, that's one thing, and no one but you can decide that. But if you're hiding in here because you're afraid, well, I never took you to be a coward."

Aiza blinked, stung. "I'm not a coward."

"I know. So don't act like one."

"Well, why do you think he's waiting for *me*?"

"He's obviously smitten with you. He asks me about you all the time. I finally told him it doesn't really matter what I think; all that matters is what he thinks. And what *you* think."

"I miss him," Aiza said. "After everything I lost, some of which I'll never get back, he's the only thing I miss. I thought I lost this place forever. But here I am, in my office, holding my nephew, and I'm missing him."

Stephanie carefully scooped the baby from Aiza's arms. "Then don't be afraid. You can't hide behind the pup forever."

"Right. Okay. God, why don't I keep a bottle of whiskey back here? Well, wish me luck."

"Yeah, break a leg," Stephanie said with a wry smile.

Aiza found Noah quickly; he was talking to Seth and Sera, his date at his side. The woman said something and she felt a flash of recognition: it was Dana. Her hair had grown longer and was now a darker shade; she was in a well-cut dress instead of a business suit, but it was definitely her, and the earlier jealousy was definitely out of line. Aiza rolled her eyes and wondered when she'd regressed to being a thirteen-year-old.

She squared her shoulders and moved in their direction, pausing long enough to whisper to Cyn that Stephanie was watching the baby in the office and maybe she would enjoy a bit of company. Cyn turned an interesting shade of pink but she didn't lose any time scurrying behind the bar.

The closer she got to Noah, the more her stomach dipped and fluttered. She knew it was ridiculous to be nervous, but she couldn't seem to get the butterflies under control. It was almost enough to make her want to turn around, but Dana saw her before she had the chance to change her mind and waved her over.

"Aiza! I didn't get a chance to say hi earlier. How are you? How have you been?"

"I'm great. It's wonderful to see you again."

"Well, I hope y'all don't think of me as a party crasher, but when Noah told me the women who brought down the Wolf Brotherhood would both be here, I insisted he bring me."

"That's flattering but..."

"There you are!"

Aiza turned around and walked into her brother's very enthusiastic embrace.

"Oh my God, Aiza, it's so good to see you."

"Oh, Steve. I'm sorry, I should have called." It never occurred to her to call her brother. She'd never been particularly close to the golden child, and now she was surrounded by him.

"Oh, hey, I understand. Things must have been very hectic for you. Here, this is my wife Jessica, our sons Rob and Chris, and our new daughter, Cecelia."

He wasn't even finished speaking before they swarmed around her with eager, friendly hugs. The kids seemed cute enough, but her attention was drawn to Noah, and their eyes met over the kids' heads.

He must have been able to read her mind, because he stepped forward with a friendly smile. "Hi, I'm Noah Longtail. It's a pleasure to meet you." He shook each hand in turn, made some courtesy small talk with Jessica, and then took Aiza by the elbow. "I hope you all don't mind if I steal her for a minute? I need her help to make a special cocktail."

"Special cocktail?" Aiza asked under her breath as he led her away. "Is that a come on?"

"If you want it to be."

"Oh look, we're out of champagne. Let's go find some." Aiza shifted, guiding him to the dark, quiet keg room.

As soon as the door closed behind them, he drew her against him and claimed her mouth with a kiss that had her toes curling and her mouth opening in shock. He took advantage of the way her lips parted, and she thought maybe she should protest, but as the kiss deepened, she forgot all about that. After all, this had been what she wanted, what she'd been thinking about and too afraid to acknowledge.

"I'm sorry," he said, breaking away. "I'm sorry. I shouldn't have done that. I just—"

"Oh, Noah. Shut up."

She drew her mouth back to his, sighing with pleasure at the taste and smell of him. The party outside was as loud as ever, but that had dulled to a vague din beneath the sound of her beating heart. She slid her fingers through his hair and down his neck, over the breadth of his shoulders, itching to feel more of him; to feel his skin and muscles and the soft hair that covered his chest and abs.

"God, Aiza."

He hiked the skirt of her cotton sundress up to her waist, exposing her thighs and hips. Her hands moved down his body and found the outline of his thick cock. It strained against his trousers and she was all too happy to pull the zipper down and free him from the restrictive material. He gasped as she folded her fingers around his shaft, and she felt a little dizzy, a little delirious from the sudden wave of pleasure moving down her spine.

"I need you," he moaned against her mouth and she couldn't do anything but nod as he lifted her off the ground. Her legs wrapped around his hips and he nudged past her panties, seeking the heat of her body. The sensation of his satin-smooth skin sliding over her slick flesh made her whimper and she felt him smile. "Not yet, baby. Not yet." He guided himself to her opening and pushed himself into her tight channel. Her whimper instantly transformed into a shout for more, barely muffled against his lips.

She'd always enjoyed sex, but she never felt anything quite like this—her body so attuned to another person, so sensitive and needful. Aiza clung to him, her nails digging into his shoulders, her back scraping against the wall with every hard thrust. It wasn't long until her eyes were completely back in her head and she was unmindful, entirely unaware of her moans, shouts, and pleas.

But the keg room was far from soundproof, and the music was loud, but not so loud that Sera didn't pick up on the strange noises with her newly-enhanced ears. Seth heard it, too, and was unable to hide his smirk.

"Hopefully, Noah will lighten up now."

Sera laughed. "Has he been that bad?"

"He's been insufferable. Either talking about her or brooding over her and driving us crazy. What about Aiza?"

"She never said a word."

Seth snorted. "Your sister doesn't share much, does she?"

"No, no she does not." Sera folded her fingers around her husband's and smiled. "Have I told you how handsome you look tonight?"

"Yes. Did I mention how beautiful you are?"

"A few times."

"Or how happy you make me?" Seth asked, bringing her mouth to his lips and tenderly kissing each knuckle.

"Once or twice."

He gave her a slow smile that sent a chill down her spine. "Or how much I want to get you alone?"

"We've still got the cake...and the first dance..."

"Stephanie has the baby for the night. Everybody else is already drunk. They won't notice if we slip out for a minute."

"Well, they'll notice," Sera said dryly, "but I have a feeling you don't care."

"Not at all. Do you?"

"Not even a little bit. Let's go." Sera led Seth along the perimeter of the tavern, scooting behind the bar and pausing at the closed office door. "Maybe we should tell Stephanie—"

"Wait."

"What?"

He cocked his head. "Listen. I don't think she's alone in there."

Sera frowned and listened until she heard the unmistakable sound of soft whimpers and rhythmic moans. "Oh my God. Everybody's getting lucky except us!"

"We can change that. Come on."

"Can you hear Charlie?"

He paused for a moment to listen, sharpening his keen auditory senses and nodded, "Yes, he's sleeping." He kissed the back of her hand again. "Let's go."

Laughing, she followed her husband into the shadows and melted into the heat of his embrace.

THE END

Meg Ripley is an author of steamy shifter romances. A Seattle native, Meg can often be found curled up in a local coffee house with her laptop.

FREE BOOK SERIES!

Download Meg's entire *Caught Between Dragons* series when you sign up for her newsletter!

Sign up by visiting Meg's Facebook page: https://www.facebook.com/authormegripley/